"I like women with fire in their eyes and a go-to-hell attitude."

Max allowed himself just one touch of her hair. "I like them with shining black hair and legs so long they make you want to fall to your knees and thank God you're alive."

Damn it, her heart had shifted again. Now it was in her throat, making it hard to breathe. Still, Lily raised her chin defiantly. Willing him to do something to prove her wrong.

"I don't believe you."

He shrugged as if it made no difference to him one way or another.

"Believe what you want. But, woman, you have stirred up something inside of me I've never felt before and I think that for both our sakes, we should walk away from this here and now, before we both do something that there'll be no walking away from...."

Dear Reader,

This May, we celebrate Mother's Day and a fabulous month of uplifting romances. I'm delighted to introduce RITA® Award finalist Carol Stephenson, who debuts with her heartwarming reunion romance, *Nora's Pride*. Carol writes, "*Nora's Pride* is very meaningful to me, as my mother, my staunchest fan and supporter, passed away in May 2000. I'm sure she's smiling down at me from heaven. She passionately believed this would be my first sale." A must-read for your list!

The Princess and the Duke, by Allison Leigh, is the second book in the CROWN AND GLORY series. Here, a princess and a duke share a kiss, but can their love withstand the truth about a royal assassination? We have another heart-thumper from the incomparable Marie Ferrarella with *Lily and the Lawman*, a darling city-girl-meets-small-town-boy romance.

In *A Baby for Emily*, Ginna Gray delivers an emotionally charged love story in which a brooding hero lays claim to a penniless widow who, unbeknownst to her, is carrying *their* child.... Sharon De Vita pulls on the heartstrings with *A Family To Come Home To*, in which a rugged rancher searches for his family and finds true love! You also won't want to miss Patricia McLinn's *The Runaway Bride*, a humorous tale of a sexy cowboy who rescues a distressed bride.

I hope you enjoy these exciting books from Silhouette Special Edition—the place for love, life and family. Come back for more winning reading next month!

Sincerely,

Karen Taylor Richman
Senior Editor

Please address questions and book requests to:
Silhouette Reader Service
U.S.: 3010 Walden Ave., P.O. Box 1325, Buffalo, NY 14269
Canadian: P.O. Box 609, Fort Erie, Ont. L2A 5X3

Marie Ferrarella

LILY AND THE LAWMAN

Silhouette®

SPECIAL EDITION™

Published by Silhouette Books

America's Publisher of Contemporary Romance

To
Julie Barrett,
Welcome to the fold

SILHOUETTE BOOKS

ISBN 0-373-24467-3

LILY AND THE LAWMAN

Copyright © 2002 by Marie Rydzynski-Ferrarella

Books by Marie Ferrarella in Miniseries

ChildFinders, Inc.
A Hero for All Seasons IM #932
A Forever Kind of Hero IM #943
Hero in the Nick of Time IM #956
Hero for Hire IM #1042
An Uncommon Hero Silhouette Books
A Hero in Her Eyes IM #1059
Heart of a Hero IM #1105

Baby's Choice
Caution: Baby Ahead SR #1007
Mother on the Wing SR #1026
Baby Times Two SR #1037

Baby of the Month Club
Baby's First Christmas SE #997
Happy New Year Baby! IM #686
The 7lb., 2oz. Valentine Yours Truly
Husband: Optional SD #988
Do You Take This Child? SR #1145
Detective Dad World's Most
   Eligible Bachelors
The Once and Future Father IM #1017
In the Family Way Silhouette Books
Baby Talk Silhouette Books
An Abundance of Babies SE #1422

Like Mother, Like Daughter
One Plus One Makes Marriage SR #1328
Never Too Late for Love SR #1351

*The Pendletons
Baby in the Middle SE #892
Husband, Some Assembly Required SE #931

Those Sinclairs
Holding Out for a Hero IM #496
Heroes Great and Small IM #501
Christmas Every Day IM #538
Caitlin's Guardian Angel IM #661

Two Halves of a Whole
The Baby Came C.O.D. SR #1264
Desperately Seeking Twin Yours Truly

The Cutlers of the Shady Lady Ranch
(Yours Truly titles)
Fiona and the Sexy Stranger
Cowboys Are for Loving
Will and the Headstrong Female
The Law and Ginny Marlow
A Match for Morgan
A Triple Threat to Bachelorhood SR #1564

*The Reeds
Callaghan's Way IM #601
Serena McKee's Back in Town IM #808

*McClellans & Marinos
Man Trouble SR #815
The Taming of the Teen SR #839
Babies on His Mind SR #920
The Baby beneath the Mistletoe SR #1408

*The Alaskans
Wife in the Mail SE #1217
Stand-In Mom SE #1294
Found: His Perfect Wife SE #1310
The M.D. Meets His Match SE #1401
Lily and the Lawman SE #1467

*Unflashed series

MARIE FERRARELLA

earned a master's degree in Shakespearean comedy and, perhaps as a result, her writing is distinguished by humor and natural dialogue. This RITA® Award-winning author's goal is to entertain and to make people laugh and feel good. She has written over one hundred books for Silhouette, some under the name Marie Nicole. Her romances are beloved by fans worldwide and have been translated into Spanish, Italian, German, Russian, Polish, Japanese and Korean.

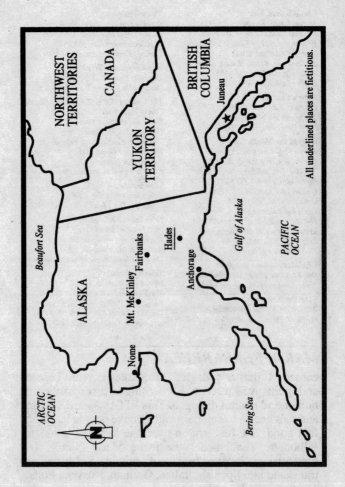

ARCTIC OCEAN

N

ALASKA

Beaufort Sea

Nome

Mt. McKinley

Fairbanks

Hades

Anchorage

Bering Sea

Gulf of Alaska

PACIFIC OCEAN

YUKON TERRITORY

NORTHWEST TERRITORIES

CANADA

BRITISH COLUMBIA

Juneau

All underlined places are fictitious.

Chapter One

"I hate men. I hate tall men, I hate short men, I hate old men, I hate young men. I hate men!"

Alison Quintano held the phone away from her ear for a moment. Distance hardly muted her older sister Lily's tirade. It was as if the petite woman who had dominated a large portion of Alison's childhood was standing right here in Hades's lone medical clinic rather than far away, in her own trendy Seattle apartment.

"You. Men. Hate. Got it," Alison quipped, trying to get Lily's voice down to a level that didn't threaten to shatter her eardrum. Lily had called her about three minutes ago and had been carrying on like this from the moment she'd answered the phone. "Now calm down and tell me what brought this on."

Even as she said it, Alison had a sneaking suspicion she knew what the problem was. Or rather, who.

Lily steamrolled right over the question, not hearing her sister. She was just too angry and trying very, very hard not to be hurt. But the pain was there, hot and biting.

How could she have been this blind?

"I especially hate sneaky plastic surgeon men."

Ah, now they were getting to it, Alison thought. Lily's fiancé, Allen, was a plastic surgeon. Alison felt guilty over the sense of relief she was experiencing. But it was there nonetheless. She had never liked Allen. None of them had.

"Does this mean the wedding's off?" Alison could just see their older brother, Kevin, doing a little jig.

Of the three of them, Kevin, who had raised them ever since their father had died, had disliked Allen the most. The artificial surgeon was the way he referred to Allen whenever he mentioned the man to the rest of them.

But, Lily being Lily, none of them had said anything to her. It would have only made her dig in her heels. Now, it looked as if her heels had been naturally dislodged.

It was hard for Alison to keep from cheering.

Feeling like a caged animal, Lily paced the length of her kitchen, a headset sitting like an appendage on her straight black hair. Normally, being around the various state-of-the-art appliances in her kitchen soothed her. But nothing was soothing her now. Short of filleting her fiancé.

Ex-fiancé, she amended with a vengeance. How could he? How *could* he?

"Not only is the wedding off, but I very nearly came close to taking his head off, as well." She huffed angrily, struggling to keep the skewering feeling of betrayal at bay. "Not that he needs his head since he seems to rely very heavily on the Braille system of doing things."

With the telephone wedged against her shoulder and her ear, Alison tallied up a bill for the burly miner who had just walked out of examining room one. It took her a second to decipher her brother Jimmy's illegible handwriting. Even for a doctor it was awful, she thought.

"Does this come with any subtitles, Lily, or am I going to have to figure out what you're talking about on my own?"

Alison's words bounced off Lily's brain like so many cascading beads. Nothing was making sense right now. Lily looked around her, searching for a way to siphon off some of the anger she was feeling.

It was as if she were a kettle with the top about to blow.

She'd never been so angry in her life. Never. She'd given that narcissistic idiot some of the best entrées of her life.

Taking a breath, she tried to begin at the beginning. "Allen kept complaining about how predictable I was, how all I ever thought about was work, that I was never spontaneous." Lily ground her teeth together, thinking what a fool she'd been. Had this kind of thing really been going on under her nose all the time? "So I was spontaneous. I got Arthur to take over for me at *Lily's*, grabbed a bottle of our finest champagne from the wine cellar, packed a picnic lunch of nothing less than my finest fare and came over to his apartment to surprise him."

Finding herself in the living room without the slightest idea how she got there, Lily sank down onto the sofa as if all at once all the air had been let out of her body.

"I surprised him, all right. In bed with one of his former patients. The breast enhancement one." She spat the words out. There was no comfort in the fact that the woman had looked as though she'd been wearing a flotation device.

Lily blinked. Were those tears she felt on her lashes? No, damn it, she wasn't going to waste tears on that jerk. "He was trying to get closer to his work, no doubt."

Handing the miner his receipt, Alison nodded as the man paid her and took his leave. Poor Lily, she thought. But thank God the so-called gift to the medical profession wasn't going to be part of the family, after all. "I get the picture, Lil."

Lily tossed her head and then grabbed the headset as it threatened to slide off. "Well, picture him and his cutie wearing the lobster Newburg I threw at them."

Alison knew her sister was very capable of pitching things when she got angry. She laughed, tickled as she envisioned the sight. "Good for you. I never liked Allen anyway."

Frowning, Lily stood up and began to pace again. To think of all the time she'd wasted on that man... "Well, you don't have to try to like him anymore. The wedding is off." She blew out a long breath, feeling empty and trying not to. Where had all this sadness come from suddenly? "My life is off."

Alison knew a dramatic tirade in the making when she heard one. She tried to head her off before Lily picked up another full head of steam. "Lily."

Standing beside her audio system, Lily flipped a switch. The song playing on the radio had memories attached to it. Bitter ones now. Lily flipped the switch off again. "I should have never thought that I could give love a try."

Alison tried again. "—Lily."

"Men are scum, anyway," Lily declared like a scientist at the end of a long, carefully controlled experiment. And then she realized who she was talking to. "Your husband and our brothers excepted, of course. But in general, Aly, all men are."

"—Lily—"

"And on the whole, I'm better off without any of them in my life. If I need any spice, I can find it waiting for me on the rack—"

"Lily!"

Her sister's voice finally penetrating, Lily stopped in midstride. Alison's voice echoed in her head. "What?"

Finally. Blowing out a breath, Alison made her

pitch while indicating that the patient who had just entered should take a seat. "Why don't you come up for a vacation?"

"Come up?" Taking a vacation was as rare for Lily as taking a bath was for a cat. She paused to let the idea sink in. It didn't. It floundered. "Come up where?"

"Here." There was no response. "Where I live. Where Jimmy lives," Alison added for good measure. "We haven't seen you since forever." Or, more precisely, since her wedding to Luc. Lily had been unable to attend their brother's marriage to April Yearling last year. Now that Lily's wedding was off, there was no telling when they would see her again. She knew Lily had a tendency to lose herself in her work. "Maybe you need to get away."

The idea of getting away was not completely without appeal for Lily. But people took vacations to exciting places, not places that brought to mind an abundance of ice. "To Alaska?"

"To family," Alison told her quietly but firmly.

Lily caught her lower lip between her teeth, working it slowly as she thought. It was one of the unconscious habits she and her sister shared.

"I have Kevin." Kevin was the only one of the family who still lived in Seattle. It seemed that Hades, Alaska, population of five hundred or so, was slowly wooing the Quintanos away from their native Seattle. Or at least the younger ones.

Alison saw no problem with that. "So bring him."

It was always wonderful to see Kevin. With ten

years between them, Kevin was like a second father to Alison and she loved him dearly. Leaving Kevin behind when she moved here was the hardest thing she had ever done. Loving Luc was the easiest.

Lily laughed shortly. She wasn't the only workaholic in the family. Kevin's devotion to work had begun out of necessity, to provide for her and the others. But once they were all out on their own, Kevin, who had made the decision years ago to turn his back on beginning a family of his own to provide for the one he already had, just kept on working, running his own taxi service.

"Yeah, like I could get our older brother to go anywhere. Men just don't—"

Alison didn't have time to listen to an encore. Mrs. Newhaven had just walked in, all eight months' pregnant of her.

"Lily, I have to get back to work." She heard her sister sigh. She hated to leave her hanging like this. "I can be much more sympathetic in person, really. Take a couple of weeks off and come up here. You were going to take two weeks off for your honeymoon, right?"

Lily closed her eyes, battling sorrow, regret and searching for a fresh wave of anger to hold on to. As long as she was angry she couldn't cry. "You're not exactly who I was planning to spend those two weeks with."

Alison was ready for her. "I'm nicer than a two-timing weasel, right?"

Lily sighed, then laughed sadly. "Right."

"Then it's settled." For once, she was going to order her sister around, not vice versa. Lily's problem, Alison knew, was that she was a commando in high heels. Allen had been the first man she hadn't been able to boss around, but that was probably because he'd had his own agenda and hadn't paid attention to anything she'd said. "Make arrangements. Jimmy or I will come to the airport to pick you up and bring you to Hades."

"Hades." Lily repeated the improbable name of the small town that had lured two-thirds of her family. "The place sounds more like heaven after what I've been through."

Alison smiled, confident that Dr. Allen Ripley was undoubtedly worse for the encounter with her sister during her surprise visit. Lily's wrath was legendary when unleashed. Not that he hadn't deserve it.

"My point exactly. C'mon, Lily. We miss your smiling face."

Even as she heard her sister say it, a smile began to form on Lily's lips. She'd been incredibly busy, making *Lily's* one of the trendiest places in Seattle. But even at the height of her success, there was an emptiness she tried to ignore. She had to admit she did miss her siblings. "Not to mention my cooking."

Alison laughed. There was no denying that. No one on earth could cook like Lily.

"Not to mention your cooking," she agreed. The door to the clinic opened again and two more patients walked in. Even though it was almost evening, it looked as if she and Jimmy were going to be here well past closing. Again. "Now, I really have to go. Promise me you'll come." Alison paused, waiting. "Promise."

Lily took a deep breath, then released it. Maybe she did need to get away for a while. Really get away. Not just from the memory of the man she'd thought she was going to spend her future with, but from everything. She'd been working almost nonstop ever since she'd opened *Lily's* more than five years ago. The restaurant was doing great.

The same, unfortunately, couldn't be said for her. Maybe it was time to change that. "Okay, I'll come."

Alison breathed a sigh of relief. "Wonderful. I'll call you tonight, we'll make arrangements and get you booked on a flight up here as soon as possible."

Her sister, as she remembered, never walked when she could run. A smile curved Lily's mouth fondly. "Don't waste time, do you?"

"Nope." There was genuine affection in Alison's voice. "I learned from the best." She rose as she saw Mrs. Newhaven's hand go limp. She'd just been fanning herself. The woman's eyes started to roll up toward her head. "Gotta go. 'Bye."

The line went dead.

Lily felt at her waist where the telephone receiver was attached. She pressed the off button. Even as she did so, a fresh wave of sadness came sweeping in, threatening to undo her.

It wasn't that she loved Allen with her dying breath, she knew she didn't. She'd thought they went well together and, on paper, he was all the things she'd thought she wanted in a man. Handsome, successful, intelligent. Somewhere along the line, though, she must have missed the part about being a lying cheat. So she'd cut him loose, her pride smarting somewhat.

It was just that…just that she felt alone. Again. And every so often, being alone had sharp edges to it that hurt.

Enough of this self-pity, Lily upbraided herself, annoyed. She had her restaurant, her reputation and her career. And a family who loved her. Not everyone was nearly so lucky.

Squaring her shoulders, Lily marched over to the piano and the framed photograph of Allen. He'd given it to her on her last birthday with an inscription. The Best For The Best.

Should have been a clue, Lily. Should have been a clue…

Taking the photograph in hand, Lily escorted it to the kitchen where she threw it, frame and all, into the trash. Glass shattered as it hit the side of the metal container on its way to the bottom. It was a satisfying sound.

Lily felt marginally better as she went to pack.

Max Yearling passed his hand over the rim of the tanned hat in his hand as he looked around the vast airport, trying to spot a woman he only vaguely remembered meeting once several years ago.

He wasn't sure just how he'd gotten roped into this. As a rule, he didn't like to fly and only did so as a last resort. If God had really meant men to fly, He would have made them with feathers instead of hair.

But April didn't ask for much and she had asked for this, so he'd said yes.

It wasn't as though he could hide behind the fact that he was busy. He wasn't. Being sheriff of Hades and its surrounding territory had its busy times, but today wasn't one of them. Most times, the job involved a great number of small tasks and duties that most people would find monotonous.

But he didn't. Not usually. There was comfort in the familiar and he never looked down his nose at any part of his job. Not even looking under the Widow Anderson's bed to assure her that no one had sneaked into her home, waiting to have their way with her once she was asleep.

All of eighty-one, the widow had a healthy imagination, he thought, smiling to himself. A little like his own grandmother's, except that Ursula Hatcher, Hades's postmistress for as long as anyone could remember, would probably have been delighted to have a man stashed under her bed, waiting for the lights to go out. At seventy-two, having buried three husbands and on the lookout for a fourth, his grandmother was the youngest woman he knew.

Not that there were all that many women to know in Hades, he mused, scanning faces as a fresh wave of passengers made its way into the baggage claim area. Men outnumbered women seven to one in the town he was born in. He knew that if he were to ever have that family he occasionally thought about, he was going to have to go to one of the real cities in Alaska to find a wife.

Didn't seem likely, though. In his heart, he sincerely doubted that any woman from a city larger than a bread box would want to transplant herself to a place like Hades, where people and time seemed to move in slow motion for the most part, barring earthquakes, fires and cave-ins at the local mine, the industry that employed two-thirds of the male population.

Oh, sure, Sydney, Marta, and Alison had all come from outside the state and wound up marrying local men, but they were exceptions. And most of the home-grown women were on their way out the second they reached their eighteenth birthday. Even his own sister hadn't been able to wait to get away. The only reason April had returned at all was that their grandmother had gotten ill and neither he nor June had been able to give her the full-time attention that April felt she needed. It had been April's intention to stay for no more than two weeks, the time necessary to talk their grandmother into having heart surgery. Instead, she'd fallen in love and married the visiting heart surgeon, Alison's brother, Jimmy.

Funny how things arranged themselves, Max thought, shifting from foot to foot as he waited beside Sydney Kerrigan, the wife of Hades's first resident doctor. Sydney had been one of the women who had come from somewhere else to be here. And, like him, Sydney was happy to remain here for the rest of her life. She'd even learned to fly her husband's plane to help bring in supplies. For a while there, Dr. Kerrigan's plane had been the only one making trips in and out. But now there were two planes and three pilots in the immediate vicinity.

Yup, he thought, his lips curving in amusement, Hades was growing up. If not by leaps and bounds, then by hops and skips, but it was happening. Fast enough to suit him.

What wasn't happening fast enough to suit him was Lily Quintano's appearance.

"You see her?" he asked Sydney impatiently, glancing down at the photograph Alison had given him of her sister.

He wished Alison or Jimmy were here in his place. Both Alison, who was the only nurse in town, and Jimmy, referred to by the locals as "the doctor who had come on vacation only to remain," were tied up in an unexpected surgery. Neither had been able to get away to pick up their sister, thus Jimmy's call to April, who in turn had called him.

His sister was busy working against some deadline or other, snapping pictures of melting snow for some magazine and pretending it was work.

Someday, he thought, he was going to learn how to say no.

Flying out of Hades into Anchorage Airport to be the unofficial welcoming committee for a woman reputed to be a man-hating workaholic wasn't exactly his idea of a good way to spend an afternoon.

"Someone from the family has to be there," April had insisted when he'd challenged her as to why Sydney wasn't sufficient to welcome Lily Quintano and bring her back to town.

"But she doesn't know me from Adam," he'd protested fruitlessly. As far as he could remember, he'd only caught a glimpse of her at Alison and Luc's wedding. If not for the photograph in his hand, he wouldn't have been able to identify her at all.

"She will as soon as she looks into those beautiful green eyes of yours, little brother," April had assured him.

He really should have said no, he thought now, but there hadn't been anything else more pressing to do. His investigation of Jeffords's broken traplines was going nowhere at the moment and he'd thought, recklessly, that maybe a plane ride in the single-engine Cessna would clear his head. Besides, April, only eleven months his senior, knew how to nag better than any woman he'd ever met. When it came to April, he'd learned a long time ago that it was easier just to say yes.

Sydney shook her head in response to his question. And then suddenly she caught hold of his arm, pointing. "Over there, the woman in the red leather coat next to the baggage carousel. Is that—"

Max looked to where Sydney was pointing, then glanced down at the photograph. It was hard to decide. The woman in the photograph was smiling. The woman in the red leather coat was definitely not. Even at this distance, she reeked of impatience. She was frowning as she scanned the area.

Frown or not, Max had to admit that he'd never seen a finer-looking woman.

"Only one way to find out," he told Sydney, pocketing the photograph. "Wait here."

Still holding his hat in his hand, Max made his way through the crowded terminal to the baggage claim area. The closer he got, the finer the dark-haired woman looked. In the absolute sense. Given his preference, he preferred women who smiled.

He noted that, unlike a lot of passengers, the woman was dressed almost formally, wearing a light gray suit beneath her open coat. She had on what appeared to be three- or four-inch heels, which gave her the appearance of height.

She was a slight woman, he realized, with fine features and the greatest set of legs he'd ever seen.

"All the better to grind men into dust," he'd once heard from Jimmy. Her brother ought to know, Max thought.

There were a lot of men in Hades who could be led around by the nose by someone like Lily Quintano. He was going to have to watch this one—which wouldn't be all that much of a hardship, he decided as he placed himself in front of her.

"Ms. Quintano?"

Lily spun around, all but colliding with the tall, broad-shouldered man in the sheepskin jacket. As the jacket moved, she caught sight of the badge pinned to his shirt. "Yes?"

The woman knew how to cut people down into tiny

pieces, he thought, judging by the way she looked at him. "You might not remember me—"

Lily prided herself on having one hell of a memory. She remembered every single recipe she'd ever read. "Sheriff Max Yearling, April's brother. Yes, I remember you," she said in a crisp tone. "You were at Alison's wedding. So was I."

It suddenly occurred to her why the sheriff might be here in her sister's place. Lily looked beyond his shoulder. Alison was nowhere to be seen. Neither was their brother. An uneasiness struck.

"What's wrong?" she demanded, firing the words at him point-blank. "Has something happened to Alison and Jimmy?"

He could almost see the thoughts ricocheting in her head from one spot to another. She talked like she danced. Quickly. He recalled seeing her dancing at the wedding. At the time, she'd been on the arm of a very self-absorbed-looking male. Her fiancé, he'd been told. The only opinion he'd formed at the time was that she could have done better, but then, it hadn't been any of his business.

"There was an emergency at the clinic and they couldn't get away, so they asked me to come and bring you back."

She wondered if he made it sound as though he were fetching a package on purpose, then decided that she was probably giving the man too much credit.

She took the measure of him now. Handsome. Probably used that to his advantage. She wondered how many women he was stringing along, then remembered that Hades didn't have that many to string.

"They were afraid I'd get back on the plane?" she finally asked.

She was scrutinizing him. Was she planning on dissecting him? he wondered, half amused. "Something like that."

The next moment, Sydney came up to join them. Sydney had never been one to stand on ceremony and her years as the doctor's wife out here had only served to make her more gregarious. She embraced Lily warmly.

"Welcome back."

Stunned, her arms pinned to her sides, Lily pulled her head back and looked at Sydney. The other woman made it sound as if she was returning after a long journey rather than visiting for a short while to pull the unraveling ends of her life together.

All things considered, Lily supposed that the hug was appreciated. Awkwardly, she raised her arms and hugged Sydney back, her eyes on Max.

"So, has transportation improved any since the last time I was out here?"

"We've replaced some parts in the plane," Sydney told her amicably. "And since this is summer, there is a road you can use with an all-terrain vehicle. But in the winter, the road becomes impassable and there's still no way in or out of Hades except by dogsled or plane."

Lily nodded. She was just making conversation. She knew exactly what to expect, thanks to Alison.

"Sounds perfect," she answered. "Right now, I could do with a little seclusion and a lot of peace and quiet."

But even as she said the words, she wasn't all that sure she meant them. A big-city girl all of her life, Lily was already feeling homesick for the sound of traffic—of blaring horns, impatient drivers and raised voices.

And they hadn't even left the terminal yet.

Maybe, she thought as Max went to get her luggage, she'd made a mistake in coming here.

Chapter Two

Max smiled to himself. He'd been observing Alison's older, successful sister since they'd gotten airborne ten minutes ago. Judging by her frozen stare and the way she clutched her left armrest, Max figured that Lily Quintano reacted to flying much the way he did.

"I don't like it, either."

Startled, Lily turned her head away from the vast expanse of nothingness right beneath her and almost bumped into the sheriff. He was sitting much too close, but she supposed that wasn't entirely his fault. The plane was crammed, to say the least.

Right now, he seemed to be using up all her available air.

"Like what?" She wanted to know.

Max nodded around him. "Riding in a small, single-engine plane. I keep waiting for a giant hand to reach right out of the sky and bat the plane to the ground, like in those cartoons they used to have for kids." He glanced toward Sydney, who was sitting in front in the pilot's seat. "No offense, Sydney."

Sydney laughed lightly, knowing exactly how he felt. That had been her reaction once, too. "None taken. I wasn't thrilled with my first ride to Hades, either. I was sure this plane was going to go down like a stone."

Eventually, though, she'd changed her mind and managed to talk Shayne into giving her flying lessons. Lucky thing, too, otherwise she would have never been able to fly him to the hospital when he'd come down with appendicitis. She'd gotten him there just as it ruptured. Saving his life was a handy thing to hold over your husband's head when discussions got a little heated.

"You feel better about it when you're at the controls." Sydney glanced over her shoulder. It wouldn't hurt to have a few more pilots in Hades. Or a few more planes, for that matter. God knew, there were enough demands on her time these days. What Hades needed was a professional pilot who did nothing else, not like the rest of them. "Maybe you should take lessons, Max. I'd be happy to—"

He was already shaking his head. Air was not what he considered to be his natural environment.

"Thanks just the same," Max told her. "I like having my feet firmly planted on the ground. I only fly when it's absolutely unavoidable.''

Lily looked at him. That didn't make sense to her. ''So why did you volunteer to come meet my plane?''

''I didn't come to meet your plane, I came to meet you.'' He had no idea why it tickled him to correct her. Maybe because he could see that it irritated her, and he had a feeling that Ms. Lily Quintano was far too uptight for her own good. ''And it wasn't so much a case of volunteering as being volunteered.''

''Oh.''

Well, that was putting her in her place, Lily thought. Nothing like being regarded as a burden. Maybe she would have been better off staying home. She could have made a dartboard of Allen's photograph and cleared her head that way. It would have been a lot less complicated than what she'd had to go through to make arrangements to spend two weeks away from the restaurant.

''I'm sorry to have inconvenienced you.''

The woman was blunt and she could be chillier than an Alaskan January night, Max thought. He was beginning to see why the wedding had been called off. Took a hell of a man to commit himself to the likes of Lily Quintano.

He made no apologies for her assumption. ''Just part of being a sheriff,'' he told her carelessly.

Her eyes narrowed. Now he was lumping her in with chores? Why had Alison and Jimmy sent this character? ''I thought being a sheriff was catching bad guys and keeping the peace.''

He'd wondered when she'd get around to being sarcastic. "The peace more or less keeps itself out here and our bad guy supply has pretty much dwindled out."

Max didn't bother telling her about how Sam Jeffords's traps kept being broken into and destroyed. Coming from where she did, he figured Lily would probably laugh at that being thought of as a crime. He knew it didn't occur to people who lived in a city that some people's livelihoods were still being made from setting traps and bringing in furs.

Personally, he knew he couldn't do that himself—trap an animal so that someone could wear its pelt around their shoulders—but he wasn't about to impose his own values on anyone else. Took all kinds to make the world go around. Faux fur notwithstanding, there was still a large market for animal skins. And, he supposed, on the plus side, it did keep the beaver population from multiplying and overwhelming the township.

"Then what is it that you do do?" The bright noonday sun was highlighting everything within the small cabin. The nose of the weapon he had tied to his thigh peered out of its holster, gleaming. It caught Lily's attention. "Besides polish your gun?"

He wondered if she sharpened her tongue daily on a miller's wheel or if it just maintained its edge naturally.

"A little of this, a little of that." He looked at her pointedly. "Hunt for lost tourists."

She never flinched. "Get many of those?"

"Even one is too many," he told her honestly.

It was easy to get lost out here if you weren't careful. Even people native to the area got lost on occasion. It wasn't unusual to have to organize the town
into a search party. He supposed that was what he
liked best about living in a place like Hades, knowing
that he could rely on his neighbor if he had to.

"Your brother got lost when he first came out here.
He went to the Inuit village to inoculate the children
against the flu that was going around that year. It was
the beginning of June, but a freak snowstorm hit when
he was on his way back. My sister was guiding him.
If Jimmy and April hadn't found their way to the
cabin, they would have died from exposure." He
didn't mention that, ironically, it was the cabin where
he and his sisters had lived before their mother had
retreated from reality. "This can be a very unforgiving land, Lily."

There was something almost unsettlingly intimate
about having him address her by her first name.
Maybe the altitude was making her giddy, she
thought, dismissing the odd feeling.

"If it's so unforgiving, why do you and my sister
stay?"

She wasn't even going to mention Jimmy. When
she first heard that her playboy brother had decided
to take up residence in a place that was less than a
fly speck on the map, she was rendered utterly
speechless for one of the few times in her life. She
knew that Jimmy had a good heart, and that he also
liked to have a good time. From what Alison had told

her, there was no nightlife in Hades other than the Salty Dog Saloon and a couple of movie theaters.

"Why does anyone stay?"

Max smiled to himself. If he had to explain, then she missed the point. But since she was waiting for some kind of answer, and he had a feeling she was the type who wouldn't just let something go, he said, "Like a beautiful woman, it has its allure."

She had another take on why he, at least, remained here. From the way he spoke and conducted himself, she had a feeling that he wasn't exactly a go-getter. She wouldn't have given him two minutes in her world.

"Or maybe it's easier being a sheriff here than in, say—" she looked at him pointedly "—Seattle."

If she was trying to put him on the defensive, he thought, she was going to be disappointed. "Maybe. But I wouldn't know everyone in Seattle the way I do here." He made himself comfortable in his seat, knowing they'd be landing soon. "I like knowing who I'm protecting."

The plane suddenly dipped and without thinking, Lily grabbed onto Max, jerking him toward her.

"Sorry about that." Sydney tossed the words over her shoulder. "We hit an air pocket."

Lily's heart was pounding so hard that she felt as though someone was doing a drumroll in her chest. "Felt more like the pocket hit us." With effort, Lily pulled herself together. Realizing that she was still clutching Max's forearm, she flushed and released him. It was then she saw that her nails had dug into his wrist, leaving a long, red mark. "Sorry. I didn't mean to do that."

"Nice to know." He glanced at the scratch. A small red line of blood was forming along its length, making it look angry. Digging into his pocket, he took out his handkerchief and dabbed at the line. Max raised his eyes to hers. Amusement tugged at the corners of his mouth as he deadpanned, "I guess I can always tell people you drew first blood."

Lily shifted uncomfortably in her seat. She hated acting weak. It detracted from the image she had of herself, the one she liked to project.

"I'm not usually this jumpy." Lily slid forward, her hand on the back of Sydney's seat. "How much farther is it?"

The comparison to her own children's "are we there yet?" was unavoidable, but Sydney kept that to herself. She had a feeling that Alison's sister wouldn't take kindly to being compared to a ten-year-old girl and a fourteen-year-old boy, not to mention her two-year-old toddler. But she said what every good parent who hadn't yet lost their temper said in similar circumstances.

"Almost there."

Couldn't be soon enough for her, Lily thought. "Maybe I should have just rented a car at the airport and driven to Hades myself." The thought, she realized by the look on the sheriff's face, had been uttered out loud instead of safely left in the regions of her mind where she thought she'd left it. "That way I wouldn't have inconvenienced anyone," she tacked on, hoping that would get her out of the awkward situation.

"More of an inconvenience coming out to look for you," Max informed her crisply.

She didn't like being thought of as a helpless female. She hadn't felt like a helpless female since fourth grade, back when she would have sold her soul to be part of Jenny Wellington's club. Only the most popular girls in the class belonged to it and she had pointedly been excluded. She'd realized there and then that wanting something that badly only allowed other people to have power over you. She'd made up her mind that she wasn't ever going to want anything that badly again. That with the exception of her family, nothing and no one was ever going to mean that much to her again.

Her mistake with Allen was in thinking that maybe she'd made up her mind too hastily all those years ago, that maybe she did need someone to round out her existence. Someone to start a family with.

All the more fool she, Lily thought now.

She had her family. She had Kevin and Alison and Jimmy. If she needed anything beyond that, she had the people who worked for her at the restaurant. They were a family of sorts in themselves, with her as the mother. She couldn't help wondering how they were getting along right now without her.

As if on cue, the cell phone tucked away in her suit jacket pocket rang.

The tinny noise had Max quizzically raising his brow as he looked at Lily. The woman seemed to come to life right before his eyes, the altitude and the small plane that was carrying them completely forgotten.

"My phone," she said needlessly. Digging it out, she flipped it open. "Lily."

"Lily, thank God."

She immediately recognized her assistant manager's high, whiny voice, the one he used just before he began to crumble in front of her. She'd left for the airport from the restaurant, rather than from her home. Arthur had been in charge all of four hours. What could have gone wrong so quickly?

"The fool from Bradberry's didn't deliver enough lamb chops for tonight and we have that huge private banquet at eight."

The man was a gem when he didn't get in his own way. Unfortunately, that happened all too frequently. "So, call Bradberry's and have them deliver more."

There was a slight indignant huff on the other end. "I'm not an idiot, Lily. I already did that." And then the whine replaced the indignation. "They don't have enough."

"Then find my phone book in the drawer and call Fenelli's." She gave him a second name, knowing the man needed backup at all times. "Or try Wagner's Market if they don't have any."

Lily tried to keep her temper. It was hard to believe that Arthur Knight had a degree in restaurant management. The man was good at following orders, but still lacked a great deal when it came to thinking on his own. Of course, she allowed, he'd never been given the opportunity before because, other than the two days she'd taken off for Alison's wedding, she hadn't been away from the restaurant for more than a few hours. There'd been no occasion for Arthur to have to do anything on his own.

"Wait," Arthur begged, afraid she would hang up before he found the address book.

Lily could hear the sound of a drawer being opened and then the shuffling of papers. The sound got more desperate. He had better pick up whatever he threw down, she thought, envisioning the chaos.

"It's not here."

Lily closed her eyes, summoning an image, trying to block out the fact that she was being observed. The two-bit sheriff was watching her as if she were a Saturday feature in the tiny theater she guessed he frequented.

"Left-hand side, in the back. Under the green folder," she recited.

More shuffling. "Got it!" he cried in triumph with no less verve than if he were Jason and had just secured the Golden Fleece.

"Good. Now look up the phone number and call one of them. And, Arthur," she said just as she was about to break the connection, "calm down. You can do this."

"Right," he said breathlessly. "I can do this. I can do this."

Arthur was still reciting the mantra as she bid him a crisp, "Goodbye," and terminated the connection. Placing the phone back in her pocket, she finally looked at Max. He'd been observing her the entire time she'd been on the phone.

"What?"

The woman sounded as if she were a five-star general in training. "What is it you do again?"

"I run a restaurant. My own restaurant," she felt compelled to add since it was obvious that no one had said anything to him about her.

She had no idea why it mattered that he know she wasn't just some flunky for a corporation, even though she had worked for a major insurance company for several years to save up enough money for a down payment on her restaurant.

If she was looking to impress him, she was disappointed.

Max nodded, taking the information in. "Sounds more like you're a general planning some kind of major strategy."

She didn't know if he was just making an offhanded remark or criticizing her. She didn't react well to criticism. In-law or not, she definitely hadn't made up her mind to like Sheriff Max Yearling. "Arthur needs a firm hand."

She sounded as if she were talking about a horse or a pet. It was as plain as the nose on his face that the lady liked being in control. He pitied the man who had the misfortune of falling for her face, not realizing what the total package involved.

"Arthur, your fiancé?"

Eyes widening, Lily laughed. It was the first time, she realized, since she had found Allen in bed with that former patient of his. Arthur was a dear in his own way, but definitely not someone she would even remotely think of in a romantic light. It wasn't even his tall, gawky frame or the fact that he had an Adam's apple that seemed to be in perpetual motion. It was that, quite truthfully, he was skittish of his own shadow and if ever she were to think about romance again, she wanted a man, not a mouse. Not even a tall mouse.

"Hardly. What makes you think that?"

Max lifted a shoulder carelessly, letting it drop again. "The way you were ordering him around, it sounded as if you had a relationship."

Lily stiffened her shoulders. She didn't like what he was implying. "We do. Arthur is my assistant manager."

He studied her for a moment, thinking that she was probably one of those people who hadn't a clue how to kick back. "I thought you came here to relax."

Though his voice was low, and to an outside ear, easygoing, Lily felt as if she was being interrogated. "I did."

He nodded at the pocket where she'd put her phone. "Don't you think you should turn your phone off, then?"

She looked at him as if he'd just suggested that she practice skydiving without a parachute. She'd had a cell phone on her person ever since they'd been invented. In the early days that had meant carrying around something that had resembled a talking brick.

"Why would I want to do that?"

He heard the defensive tone in her voice and knew his estimation about her inability to relax was right on the money. "So that the people who work with you can't bother you with questions."

"They don't work with me, they work for me," she corrected. "And what do you suggest I do, shut off my phone, forget about everything and after two weeks, come back to no restaurant? No thank you. I *want* Arthur to bother me with work questions if it means I have a thriving restaurant when I get back."

Max was trying to get a fix on what she was actually saying. "Then this Arthur you have running things for you while you're gone is incompetent?"

Lily became indignant. Arthur might have his failings, but no one was going to say that about him but her.

"No, of course he's not incompetent."

A smile spread along his lips slowly, like the early morning sun creeping out over the horizon. "Oh."

She didn't like the sound of that at all. "What do you mean, 'oh'?"

Again Max shrugged, pausing to look out the window before he answered. They were getting close to home. Longest run from the airport to Hades he could remember, he thought.

"Just that maybe you're afraid that this Arthur guy can get along without you." He watched her eyes. They began to darken as he spoke. "Maybe you don't want to find out that you're not as indispensable as you'd like to think you are."

She'd had just about enough of this man. She

hadn't come all this way to be ignored by her siblings and packed off with some know-it-all guy with a badge.

"Is this what you do as sheriff? Hand out homey advice?"

He saw her eyes grow darker still, like a storm coming in from the ocean. "I like to think of it as pointing people in the right direction."

"Well, your sense of direction is off, Lawman. Because my instincts are fine and I'll handle my restaurant the way I see fit, thank you very much." She could feel her anger building. "Where do you get off, telling me how to run my business?"

The louder her voice grew, the quieter his became. The way he saw it, for every storm, there had to be a calm. That was his role in the scheme of things. He rarely, if ever, lost his temper.

"Wasn't telling you how to run the restaurant, I was telling you how to relax. Something—" he cast about for a polite wording of the problem "—I don't think you quite know how to do."

When was this damn plane going to land? She wanted to get out of these close quarters, where she was confined with this man, before she forgot that she was a lady. A very tired, exasperated lady. "Not all of us are lucky enough to have found a way to make a living doing nothing."

"We're here," Sydney announced a little too brightly, hoping to prevent a major flare-up.

"Great," Lily growled.

The sooner she was away from the know-it-all

sheriff, the better. What were Alison and Jimmy thinking, sending him to accompany her? She would have sooner ridden in a cage with a boxful of tarantulas. They might have been hairier, but they would have certainly been better company. And a hell of a lot less judgmental.

The landing that came several minutes later was almost flawless, but Lily could still feel her stomach churn as the wheels touched down. The second they came to a stop, she began unbuckling her seat belt. It wouldn't give.

It figured, she thought grudgingly as she heard Sydney disembark. Frustrated, she tugged on the belt, trying to disengage the two halves.

"Stuck?"

Lily looked up to see that the know-it-all with the liquid-green eyes had not only gotten off the plane, but had rounded the rear and come to her side. To add insult to injury, he was looking down at the belt that refused to come undone.

"I can manage," she snapped.

For a second, Max debated standing back and letting her continue to struggle. But then his training got the best of him. Being a sheriff meant taking the good with the bad. This part was obviously the bad.

"Why don't you stop being superwoman and let someone help you once in a while?" Not waiting for an answer, Max moved her hands aside and took over.

She was about to swat his hands away, but her desire to get free overrode her desire to put him in his place. "Ever hear about giving someone an inch and they take a mile?"

He raised his eyes to hers and, for a moment, managed to stop the very air around them. "I don't want a mile, Lily. I don't even want the inch." The belt snapped apart. "There, you're free."

Why the air had managed to lodge itself in her lungs when he'd raised his eyes to hers just then, she had no idea.

Maybe she was a little unstable from the flight, she thought, her head slightly foggy.

"Yes," Lily heard herself saying, "I am."

As she reached for the side of the cabin, to brace herself before she took that first long step down, she felt his wide hands on her waist, his tanned, strong fingers registering one by one. The next moment, he was swinging her out of the plane and her feet were touching the ground.

It was hard working her tongue around the cotton in her mouth. "Thanks."

He touched his fingers to the brim of his hat by way of acknowledgment. "Don't mention it." Glancing at Sydney, he said, "She's all yours," with what sounded like unadulterated humor and relief.

And with that, he turned and walked away.

Lily wished that she'd come in winter instead. That way, there would have been snow on the ground and she could have made a snowball. Throwing one at his head would have made her feel a whole lot better.

Chapter Three

Lily turned back to look at Sydney. "Is he always this charming?"

Sydney smiled, taking out the single suitcase that Lily had brought with her. Funny, she would have pegged the woman for someone who packed a minimum of two suitcases just to go away for the weekend. Just showed you could never tell.

She glanced at Max's retreating back. "Pretty much."

Lily took the suitcase from her. "I was being facetious."

"I know." Sydney's grin grew wider. "I wasn't."

She led the way to her sports utility vehicle, which stood waiting for them at the end of the small runway. The airstrip was little more than a large clearing, but then, there really wasn't much need for anything more. Not until there were more airplanes in Hades than just theirs and the one that belonged to Jeb Kellogg, the former grocer's son.

Sydney opened the door on the driver's side and reached in for the trunk release. "Well, let's get you delivered."

Lily dropped her suitcase in, then came around to the passenger side. "You didn't lock your car?"

Sydney shook her head. "The only thing we lock our doors against in Hades is the wind, not each other." Getting in, she put her key into the ignition.

Lily watched the only other vehicle in the area pull away. The word Sheriff was painted on the side of the Jeep in big, bold black letters.

Black suited her mood, as well, and she wasn't altogether clear as to why. Residue from Allen, she surmised. That, and having to deal with an irritating specimen of manhood just now. "Why did he bother coming at all, I mean, if he was just going to leave like that?"

Sydney noted the way Lily was watching Max drive away. She doubted the woman even realized how interested she looked. Well, Alison's sister wouldn't be the first woman, young or old, to get hooked on the town's sexy sheriff.

Glancing in her rearview mirror for any stray animals darting into the road, Sydney put the vehicle in gear and pulled out. "Because April asked him to."

So he had indicated. She didn't like thinking of herself as an assignment, liked his thinking of her as such even less. "Does he always do everything April asks him to?"

"Whenever he can." A fond smile tugged at Sydney's lips. Since she'd come to live here five years ago, she had learned quite a bit about the people of the town. Mostly all good. "They're very close."

She debated for a moment, then decided that it wouldn't hurt for Lily to have a few facts at her disposal. It wasn't as if this was a secret, and it might help her see Max in a better light.

"From what I gather, their mother sort of drifted away into a land all her own after their father just took off one day. April was eleven, Max was ten. June was about seven, I think. Anyway, April tried very hard to be both mother and father to the others, even after her grandmother took them all in. Max feels he owes them both a lot—his grandmother and April." She spared Lily a glance as she drove into the heart of the town. "He's sensitive that way."

Lily watched the car up ahead disappear around the bend and frowned. "He certainly doesn't strike me as being the sensitive type."

"That's just Max's way. He doesn't warm up much until he gets to know you. Give him time."

There wasn't another soul around anywhere, Lily noted. This place was even more desolate than she'd remembered. No wonder she'd read that they paid people to live here. They certainly couldn't pay her enough to spend her life in Alaska.

"I don't intend to be here that long."

Sydney merely smiled to herself. She'd heard those

words before more than once. Had even thought them herself when she'd first arrived. She'd come then to marry the man who had written her such wonderful, glowing letters about the region where he lived. He'd won her heart with his beautiful prose. But when she'd deplaned in Anchorage, after pulling up stakes and packing up her entire life, she'd discovered that her almost-husband had had a change of heart. He'd run off with the woman he'd been trying to get over when he'd written all those letters to her.

It was his brother, Shayne, who'd come to the airport to give her the bad news. Feeling sorry for her, Shayne, who'd been struggling with his own loss at the time because his brother was the only other resident doctor in the area, had offered her temporary lodgings until she could book a flight back to where she'd come from.

It was a lucky thing, she thought, looking back now, that Hades hadn't had a hotel. Otherwise, she might have very well left without finding her heart. But she'd stayed with Shayne and wound up marrying him. Being jilted by his brother was the best thing that had ever happened to her, she mused.

Life had a funny way of making things work whether or not you were aware of it.

Sydney glanced at the woman beside her. Who knew what the future held for Lily? Both of her siblings had come here, intending to be in Hades for only a short while. Alison had come to earn credits toward her nurse practitioner degree by working in the town's only clinic. Jimmy had just come to visit Alison. Both had wound up falling in love with natives of Hades and putting down roots here.

"Fate's kind of funny," she told Lily, guiding her vehicle carefully along a winding road. "It doesn't really pay much attention to what you intend so much as what it intends."

It was all Lily could do to keep from closing her eyes and sighing. Another homily. Did everyone around here sound as if they had stepped out of a Norman Rockwell painting?

She sincerely hoped that living in this small, isolated Cracker Jack box-size village hadn't done a number on Alison's brain or on Jimmy's.

"I've got a life waiting for me back in Seattle. A life and a restaurant," she added. "I'm just here because it's been a long time since I've seen either Alison or Jimmy and I thought it might be time for a visit."

Lily covertly slanted a look toward Sydney to see if the woman seemed to know anything to the contrary. She didn't think Alison would have told anyone that she was coming here to get over breaking up with Allen, to somehow make peace with the fact that she had wasted three years of her life on a man who didn't have the depth of a hand mirror.

Sydney merely nodded politely, allowing the other woman to have her lie and her dignity. She knew exactly why Lily Quintano had suddenly put her extremely busy life on hold and come out here to "the wilderness," as she knew Lily referred to Hades. It wasn't an overwhelming need to see her siblings so much as to mend a bruised ego and heart, in that order.

It wasn't that unusual a reason. Her best friend, Marta, had come for the same one. To get over a man, or, more specifically, to get over what had amounted to a very bad relationship.

This was the place for it, all right. Sydney turned to the right to avoid the rabbit that bounded into the road.

"Sorry. Rabbit," she explained when Lily made a grab for the dashboard.

They had men of all sizes and shapes to spare in and around Hades, Sydney thought. Even the plainest woman could hope for more than a little ego-soothing attention, and Lily Quintano was far from plain. Her ego should be up and running in no time.

"Family's important," Sydney went on to agree. "I didn't have any when I first came out here. My father had just died and I was totally alone." She didn't bother telling Lily what had brought her to this place. That would come later, if the other woman was interested. Right now, she had a feeling it would only bore her. "But I got very lucky. I found a wonderful man and he came equipped with two children." Whom she couldn't have loved more if they were her own. They had a daughter of their own now and all three children had equal claims to her heart. "The townspeople became my extended family."

Definitely Norman Rockwell, Lily thought. She didn't belong here. She didn't need solitude, she decided. She needed someplace busy, someplace with noise to fill her head and make her forget everything else until she got over being angry that she had been such an idiot.

"This is a great place to visit—or to stay in," Sydney was saying as she pulled up to the clinic.

Lily remained where she was, looking around at the area. She'd only been here once before and the compactness of the town still amazed her. There was hardly more than a handful of streets, with buildings haphazardly scattered among them. She tried to picture what daily life would be like here for her brother and sister. Besides boring.

Alison, Lily knew, had always been self-contained, driven by a sincere desire to help others. Until she'd heard about Shayne's open plea for medical personnel, she'd been considering travelling to a Third World country to work with underprivileged children to earn her practical credits. Lily supposed that living here would almost be considered a luxury in comparison to that.

But Jimmy... Jimmy had been a different story. Her younger brother had always been footloose and fancy free. Jimmy loved the nightlife. He was almost as good at partying as he was at being a cardiac surgeon. How did he, more than Alison, stand living here in this one-horse town?

Sydney had already gotten out of the vehicle and retrieved Lily's suitcase. She now stood with it in her hand, waiting. Lily didn't seem to be moving.

"Are you coming?" Was anything wrong? she wondered. "This is where Alison and Jimmy work.

They should be all finished with the emergency that kept them from coming to meet your plane in Anchorage. Mrs. Newhaven went into early labor and was hemorrhaging,'' she explained with the matter-of-factness of a doctor's wife who had heard almost everything at least twice. "They had to do an emergency C-section.''

Hardly hearing her, Lily got out of the sports utility vehicle. She shaded her eyes against the almost-blinding sun and looked at the wooden, one-story building with its new roof and brand-new paint job.

This was it, she thought sadly. Jimmy had given up a promising career in Seattle's Community General to stitch and mend here.

Maybe it was judgmental, but she couldn't help shaking her head. She wasn't driven by the thought of accumulating a fortune—none of them were—but they'd all done without as children and each of them knew that money was always a good thing to have, to fall back on when other things blew up in your face.

How could Jimmy hope to ever achieve his full earning potential in a place that was barely the size of a postage stamp? That didn't even have a hospital, just a clinic? Could he really be happy here, or was he staying because he loved April and she wanted to stay in Hades?

Sydney laid a hand on her shoulder. "Something wrong?"

Coming to life, Lily shook her head. She didn't believe in sharing feelings with strangers and, despite

her smile and her friendly manner, Sydney Kerrigan
was a stranger. ''No, just thinking.''

And I can guess just what you're thinking. ''It's
bigger than it looks.''

Lily blinked, struggling to pull herself together. ''It
would have to be.''

Across the street, Max stood by the window in his
office. He'd walked in only a couple of minutes ago.
The red light on his answering machine had been
blinking but for once he'd chosen to ignore it, at least
for a few minutes.

He silently watched Sydney take Lily into the
clinic. He was surprised the latter wasn't struggling
to ward off a nosebleed. She was certainly holding
her head high enough to warrant one.

He supposed that she reminded him a little of the
way April had been before she'd left Hades. Maybe
even a little of the way she'd been when she'd returned. At first. He'd certainly agree that it took a
while for the town's virtues to sink in.

He bet that Lily Quintano was counting the minutes
until she got back to Seattle.

As for him, Max couldn't see himself living anywhere else.

It amazed him how two sisters could be so different. From all that he could tell, Alison was easygoing
and dedicated. Lily was wound as tight as his grand-
father's old pocket watch had been just before the
spring had popped out of it.

He couldn't help wondering what would make Lily's spring pop out of its setting.

With a shrug, he went back to his desk to play his message and to get back to the work that Alison's sister found so inconsequential.

"I don't really want a party," Lily protested later that afternoon.

Alison had taken the latter part of the day off at Shayne's insistence and taken her sister to the house she and Jean Luc shared. Jimmy had opted to pop over with them, promising Shayne to be back within the hour.

It looked now as if it might be a little longer than that, but Alison knew Jimmy didn't want to leave her with her hands full. Even if she did have Luc there with her to lean on. Lily, even in good spirits, could be overwhelming and in her present state she could roll right over everything and everyone in her path.

"I came to get away from everything, remember?" Lily reminded Alison. "Not to be hurled into the middle of it." The very last thing she wanted was to have to pretend to be having a good time amid all these backwoods people. It was different at *Lily's*. She came out of the kitchen periodically to do a little kibitzing, a little glad-handing and a fair amount of smiling, then retreated back to what she knew. Spice racks, soufflé bowls and ovens.

"No hurling, I promise." Alison raised her hand in a solemn oath.

"It'll do you good to get out amid people, Lil,"

Jimmy told her. "These are our friends." He pretended to give her a penetrating look, knowing that no one could ever really know what was going on in his sister's mind. Despite her commando ways, she played things very close to the chest. "What's the matter, Lil? You always liked being the center of attention before."

Had he been paying that little attention to her, too? "No, I always liked being in the center of *doing* things," she pointed out to her brother. "I don't like attention for attention's sake and if I go with you to this Salt Water Taffy place—"

"Salty Dog," Luc corrected, grinning. He took no offense at the slip, even though he and his cousin, Ike, were co-owners of the saloon, as they were with various others pieces of property in and around Hades. He could see that beneath the bravado his sister-in-law was one unsettled lady.

"Whatever." Lily flashed what passed as an apologetic look at Luc. She hadn't meant to insult him, it was just that she thought it was a silly name. The Salty Dog Saloon. Who *went* to places like that these days? "If I go there with you tonight, I'm going to feel as if I'm on display."

"You will be," Jimmy told her, draping his arm around Lily's thin shoulders. She looked drawn and tired, he thought, not like her old self. Alison had gotten her out here just in time. He wished he was back in Seattle for ten minutes, just long enough to do a number on the no-good bastard who'd made her suffer like this—even though he was relieved that Allen wasn't going to be part of the family after all. "We don't have that many new faces. And it's all in harmless fun." He gave her a quick one-armed hug. "C'mon, Lil, you've got to snap out of this. Allen wasn't worth it."

Lily shrugged off his arm, stepping back. She didn't like attention being brought to her mistake. "No, he wasn't, but I'm not in anything to snap out of, I just have a little jet lag, that's all."

They all knew denial when they heard it, but no one pointed out the obvious.

Still, Alison felt compelled to say, "It wasn't that long a trip, Lily. Jimmy and I have taken it enough times to know."

Boxed in, knowing that all three meant well, Lily shrugged helplessly. "All right, I'll think about it."

"Good." Alison took her hand, pulling her to the guest room. "While you're thinking, get dressed."

Digging in her heels, literally and otherwise, Lily looked down at her suit. "This isn't good enough for your friends?"

Alison exchanged looks with Luc. Lily was missing the point. "Nope, it's too good." She saw her sister raise a confused brow. "We like our comfort here in Hades. The byword is casual."

She worked seven days a week at a clip, and dressed the part of a restaurant owner. Casual didn't exist in her closet.

"Maybe I should have worn a torn pair of jeans," she said sarcastically.

Luc nodded. "Maybe."

She flushed, hoping she hadn't insulted him. She genuinely liked her sister's husband and didn't want to hurt his feelings. But she didn't want to mingle with a bunch of sex-starved miners and lumberjacks, either. That wasn't why she'd come.

She tried to present her case to Luc. "Look, all I want is a quiet evening with my brother and sister and their spouses."

Knowing that Luc had the heart of a lovable puppy when confronted with a damsel in distress, Alison decided to take over. She tugged on her sister's hand. "This'll be fun, Lily. Trust me."

But Lily wasn't going to be outmaneuvered. "If it's all the same to you—"

"Say, Lily," Jean Luc began genially, moving to her other side. "Since we are throwing this party tonight at the Salty, maybe you could help me out?"

Suspicion padded over on light cat paws. Lily raised one eyebrow. "How?"

"Well, I was thinking of making spareribs for tonight's menu—" He looked as if he was struggling with the thought. "But, you know, that hasn't been moving very well lately. Used to be a real crowd pleaser, but not anymore." He looked to her for help. "I think everyone's gotten bored with it."

In Lily's experience, nothing should remain on a menu indefinitely. And she had a pretty good idea that nothing on Ike and Jean Luc's menu had changed for the last quarter of a century. Maybe longer.

"You're probably right. You've got to spice things up, never let yourself get predictable. Menus have to change and, even if they remain the same for a while, you change the ingredients. Customers like that. The same, but different.'' Her whole demeanor changed. This was her realm and she stepped into it gladly. ''What kind of sauce have you been using?''

Luc looked at her innocently. ''I'm not sure. Something Ike whipped up.''

She nodded. Klondyke LeBlanc was the driving force behind the partnership. Luc had told her that it was Ike's vision that had gotten them rolling to begin with, but she had a feeling that the vision was severely limited when it came to things such as food.

''Something with ketchup, water and tomato paste, no doubt,'' she said under her breath. ''What time is this party?''

There was a sparkle in Lily's eyes. Luc suppressed his smile. ''Eight.''

Lily looked at her watch. ''Eight?'' That only gave them five hours to get ready. ''What are you standing around here for? We need to get started.'' Ignoring Alison and Jimmy, she was already hustling Luc toward the front door. ''How many people are you expecting?''

He gave her an honest answer. ''Hard to say. Probably most of the town'll show up at one point or other.'' All the people of Hades had to hear was the word ''party'' and they turned out in force.

Lily paused. She was vaguely aware of the fact that the population hovered around five hundred. Doing a quick calculation in her head, she began rattling off ingredients and quantities at him as she tugged him toward the front door again.

Alison knew what Lily could be like once she got going. There was no such thing as "half measure" with her sister. "Wait, Lily, we didn't invite you here to work."

"This isn't work," Luc told her innocently. "This is pitching in, right, Lily?"

Lost in the list she was making up in her head, Lily hadn't even heard the question or her sister's protest. "We're wasting time, Luc. I'm going to need an extra set of hands to peel onions."

"Why don't you go on ahead to the car? I'll be right there," he promised, pausing by the door.

Alison crossed to him and rose on her toes. "And here I thought you didn't have a devious bone in your body." She brushed a kiss against his lips. "Nice going, Svengali."

He grinned and winked. "I thought so." Then, for good measure, he cupped the back of his wife's head and kissed her in a way that aroused them both.

"Be careful she doesn't work you to death. She can be rough when she gets going," Jimmy warned him. "I'm talking about Lily this time," he added, smirking at Alison.

"Don't worry," Luc answered. "I live with Alison. I know what I'm up against."

With a huff, Alison turned on her heel to find something suitable for her sister to wear tonight. She knew she would have to bring it to the Salty because once Lily got going in the kitchen, only dynamite would dislodge her.

Lily paused. It had to be a hundred and ten degrees in here, she thought, pointing her face toward the small oscillating fan on the wall. Alison had arrived at the Salty a few minutes after she and Luc had forced her to change into a T-shirt and jeans—Alison's since she hadn't packed any. Luckily, they were the same size.

Her own curves were a little rounder than her sister's, so the fit was tight, but sufficient. She knew she would have completely melted if she'd remained in this kitchen wearing the outfit she'd arrived in.

The tight fit chafed now, but she hadn't been thinking about clothes when she allowed herself to be momentarily sidetracked and redressed. She was thinking about the temperature beneath the huge pot of sauce she was simmering.

The instant she'd walked into the small space that Ike and Luc laughingly called a kitchen, she had commandeered it with the aplomb of not an invading soldier, but a conquering one. The part-time cook that the Salty employed, Isaac, was relegated to finding and preparing vegetables and collecting the various ingredients that Lily just couldn't work without.

The sauce, complete with submerged spareribs, had been simmering for well on to three hours now.

"Here's black pepper," Isaac offered after what had been a prolonged search.

She looked at the small man in mounting exasperation. She'd already learned that the only three ingredients he was aware of were salt, salt and more salt.

"I said cayenne pepper, not black. What is it about the word 'cayenne' you don't understand?"

"Maybe he doesn't know what cayenne pepper is," Max suggested, amused. He'd been watching her for the last few minutes. The women was a whirlwind in action.

"Then he should learn or he has no business cooking," she snapped.

Hot and sweaty, ready to sink her teeth into a meaty argument—or any argument at all—Lily brushed the falling hair out of her eyes and looked up.

Her eyes widened when she saw Max standing in the doorway, scrutinizing her.

Chapter Four

Lily wiped the perspiration from her forehead, trying not to feel self-conscious. Damn the Lawman, he would come by just when she looked her worst. The man had to have radar.

"What are you doing here?"

His eyes swept over her in long, studied strokes that she could almost feel.

He took a little longer than usual. Max was accustomed to taking in everything and everyone he encountered. It was a habit learned not so much in his profession, but from living out in the wilderness. There one miscalculation could be deadly, one mistake could be the last. Alaska was a mistress that none could afford to take for granted or to underestimate, even while enjoying her.

A little, maybe, he mused, like the woman in front of him right now.

She looked better, more human, with her hair clipped back haphazardly like that. The crisp suit she'd worn on the plane was gone, as was the pricy red-leather, three-quarter-length coat. He liked the outfit she had on better. The light blue T-shirt with the daisy in the middle and the jeans, both damp with perspiration, molded themselves to her body, sticking even closer than the small size would have warranted.

The suit she'd worn earlier had only hinted at the curves she possessed. The clothes she had on now flaunted them. Max had a hunch she wasn't even aware of it or how appealing she looked.

Made him rather glad he'd finally given in to Luc's badgering and agreed to drop by the Salty instead of going with his first inclination, which was to pass. But passing would have meant insulting not only Alison and Jimmy, but Luc and April as well, which in turn would have only insulted more people. That's how it was in Hades, everyone in town was somehow connected to everyone else. It was a little like taking the bottom orange out of the pile. No matter how isolated you might think that orange was, all the other oranges always came tumbling down at your feet in the blink of an eye.

So he'd allowed himself to have his arm twisted and then, on top of that, he'd let April browbeat him into going into the kitchen to fetch the missing guest of honor, although why one of the others couldn't do it was beyond him.

Looking at her now, he wasn't all that sorry he'd been sent.

"I drew the short straw," he said in answer to the question she'd fired at him. He nodded toward the door that led into the saloon. "They sent me in to get you."

"'They'?" It couldn't have been Jimmy or Alison. They *knew* better.

"Alison, Jimmy, Luc, April." He shrugged, wondering how many names she wanted. "'They.'" He had to admit the aroma coming from Lily's general vicinity was tempting. He couldn't decide if it belonged to her or what she had cooking on the stove. "Everyone's outside, waiting to meet you."

He meant the people in the bar. She glanced back at the two giant iron pots she had simmering. Had she made enough?

"How many in an 'everyone'?"

The question and the tone behind it surprised him. Was she being shy? He wouldn't have pegged her as that, but then, he supposed bravado was the flip side of shyness. Maybe she had just been putting on a show earlier, though God knew it hadn't been for his benefit.

He shrugged in answer to her question. "Right now maybe about a hundred and fifty people. That's about all the Salty can really accommodate at one time." And even so, they were fairly stuffed in as it was. Made maneuvering around tricky. Max grinned as he considered the thought of her being shy. Shy like a cobra, probably. "Don't worry, they won't bite."

She paused to stir the closest iron pot in front of her, then dipped her ladle in for a taste. Lily blew on the tip of it, then took the tiniest bit on her tongue. Damn it, she was right. It did need cayenne pepper and that mousy little man Luc had left to help her had disappeared on her.

"They'd better," she informed him, looking around to see where Isaac had gotten to, "after all the trouble I've just gone through."

The din from the saloon was leeching into the kitchen, making it impossible to hear her. Max came closer, tilting his head slightly. "Come again?"

Was he a complete idiot? What did he think she was doing here, wearing an apron and stirring? "The sauce." She indicated the two giant pots. "Luc said he was going to make spareribs for tonight and he wasn't happy about the sauce."

She frowned as she glanced back at the unopened jars of common barbecue sauce that took up two of the pantry shelves. No wonder there wasn't any room for cayenne pepper. Luc was a terrific guy, one of the few who were, she could readily testify, but his taste buds were tragically plebeian.

She snorted distastefully. "He had a reason not to be happy."

Max crossed to the counter and picked up one of the jars. He read the label before putting it down again. "What's wrong with this? I use it myself."

She looked at him as if he's just admitted to polishing his boots with bear grease. Without realizing it, she lifted her chin and slanted her eyes as she looked at him.

"That doesn't surprise me."

The woman's tone was nothing if not smug. He had a sudden urge to drain the smugness from her. Instead, he shoved his hands into his pockets and continued regarding her.

"And what's that supposed to mean?"

Moving past him, she began to rummage through the pantry herself, hoping to unearth the elusive cayenne pepper—if there was such a thing to be had up here. She'd temporarily forgotten where she was.

She lifted a shoulder carelessly in response to his question and let it fall again. "You don't exactly strike me as someone with discerning taste."

Coming closer, Max gave her a long look that made her very aware of the fact that her T-shirt could have been a lot looser. She could almost feel his eyes traveling over her.

"That all depends," he told her slowly, "on what we're talking about."

She could feel the hairs standing up on the back of her neck. It took her a moment to push the words out of her mouth. "The subject is food."

She had beautiful eyes, he realized. He hadn't noticed that before. And her skin was as white as the snow on the summit in February. It was obvious she wasn't the outdoors type.

He felt his palms grow itchy and wasn't sure why. "If by that you mean I'm one of those people who eats to live instead of lives to eat, then yes, you're right. I'm not very discerning.''

But he was very unsettling. She needed to get him out of the kitchen and out of her way. Having him here was only muddying up her mind.

Lily dipped her ladle into the pot again. ''Come here,'' she ordered.

Mildly amused at her tone, he gave her a sharp salute, which only served to irritate her further. ''Yes, ma'am.''

''Taste.'' But as he started to do as she said, she suddenly cried, ''Stop,'' and then lightly blew on the sauce in the ladle. Satisfied that it was now the right temperature, she offered it to him again. ''You would have burned your tongue,'' she accused.

He paused before sampling. ''You know, Lily, you'd get on a whole lot better with people if everything you said didn't sound like a criticism.''

Taking her hand to steady the spoon she was holding, Max took a small taste. Expecting something mildly pleasing, he was surprised to find that his taste buds were suddenly very aroused. It felt as if there was a party going on in his mouth. He doubted that he had ever tasted anything quite so appealing.

Unconsciously, his eyes shifted to her lips, his thoughts taking him to unexpected regions. Max found himself wondering if kissing Lily would somehow result in the same overwhelmingly pleasing surprise.

Some things, though, were better left unexplored.

He nodded his approval of the sauce. "This is damn good."

Vindicated, she tossed her head, hoping he wouldn't notice that her hand had trembled just the slightest bit when his fingers had closed over it. There was something very unsettling about this man.

Just you being vulnerable and scared, Lily, nothing more, her inner voice told her. *That bastard did a number on you, stripped you of your self-esteem and it's just going to take you a while to get back on your feet again, that's all. And whatever else he is, this backwoodsman with a tin badge is a hunk.*

Her inner voice had a way of understating things, Lily thought.

"Yes," she acknowledged haughtily, "I know." She looked at her hand. He was still holding it and the ladle. "Can I have my hand back now, please?"

His eyes seemed to touch her as Max pulled back his fingers, releasing her. "Sure thing."

Suddenly oxygen-depleted, Lily took a deep breath. There just wasn't enough air in this kitchen, she thought accusingly.

"And everything I say *doesn't* sound like a criticism," she insisted. And just where did he get off, analyzing her like that? Just because he wore an official-looking piece of tin didn't give him any jurisdiction over her.

"Oh, no? Then maybe you should invest in a tape recorder so you can hear it for yourself." He saw her bristle. He might have known that she would. "You get twice as many flies with honey—"

She dropped the ladle on the counter noisily. "I'm sure there are more than enough flies around here to give credence to your theory, but I don't particularly want any of them. I'm neither a frog nor a spider, which means that I'm just not in the market for flies. I don't like flies," she said with finality, hoping that put him in his place. A place that was far away from her.

He watched as color crept up her neck and into her cheeks. It blended nicely with the whiteness. "Works with people, too. Or don't you like those, either?"

"Some," she qualified, looking at him pointedly. "I have discerning taste."

He watched the color spread along her cheeks and caught himself wanting to trace it with his fingers. The itch in his palms intensified. "Then maybe you should see about broadening your horizons."

She tossed her head, sending the clip that was holding her hair back flying.

"My horizons are just fine the way they are."

He vaguely recalled there being a line about a lady protesting too much. She most definitely wasn't fine. "Then why did you allow someone like that peacock of a surgeon you brought with you to your sister's wedding to do a number on you?"

Her eyes widened. How dare he? How *dare* he? Where did he get off asking her questions about her life, her choices?

"How…who—why—" She was too speechless to form a coherent sentence.

It didn't take a genius to fill in the blanks. "Your

brother told me. That's the how and the who. The why is that he's worried about you and he needed to share that with someone.''

Then why didn't he talk to Alison, or even Luc? Why to this man of all people? "Nobody has to worry about me.''

The more she protested, the more obvious that the opposite was true. "Oh, I'm sure it's a dirty job, but somebody has to do it. Everyone needs someone to worry about them. It's what makes the world go around.''

Unable to stand there just looking up at him, Lily turned away. There was steam rising from one of the two pots. She turned the flame even lower.

"I thought love was supposed to do that," she said sarcastically.

Max cut the distance between them to nothing. Standing behind her, he found himself intrigued by the slope of her neck, the breadth of her shoulders. She really did seem slight.

A stick of dynamite was slight, too, he reminded himself.

"Haven't you heard, caring's part of love." Reaching around her, he loosened the ties of her apron.

Lily jumped as he made contact with her and turned to face him. The stove at her back, she found herself standing much too close to Max for comfort.

She managed to dig up her voice. "What do you think you're doing?''

Max tugged on the apron strings, loosening them even more. "My job.''

Her heart began pounding wildly again. You'd think that she was running instead of standing still, having words with a Neanderthal lawman.

"Your job is to harass me?"

"No, I told you." Max smiled at her. "They sent me in to fetch you."

"And that's your job?"

Why did her heart feel as if it was about to come bursting out of her chest? She knew what this was. This was attraction, damn it. She didn't want to be attracted to this man. She didn't want to be attracted to any man, ever again, least of all one who seemed content to not be going anywhere.

Max inclined his head. "For the moment."

That made him an errand boy. "I thought you said you were the sheriff."

"I am."

If she was trying to get him to lose his temper, it was an exercise in futility. He picked his battles and his causes. Exchanging words with a pampered, stressed-out prima donna wasn't remotely on par with things that really mattered to him.

"And I told you that being sheriff entailed doing a little bit of almost everything. Around here, it means being there for the people when they need you. Right now, Alison and Jimmy need you to be outside this kitchen." He debated adding the crowning touch, then decided she should be able to handle it. "Luc just asked you for help in the kitchen to make you feel more comfortable."

She did feel more comfortable in the kitchen. You

knew what to expect when you were cooking, knew what combining certain ingredients would yield. There wasn't that aura of certainty when you mixed together a man and a woman.

Look at the mistake she'd made the one time she'd decided to forge ahead and reach for the brass ring that represented marriage and a family. She'd fallen right off the merry-go-round and gotten trampled by the horses.

But comfortable or not, she didn't like what he was implying. Her eyes narrowed into angry slits as she looked at him. "I don't need charity."

What did it take to get this woman to step off her high horse? Max had a feeling that she had the potential to be someone really nice if she gave herself half a chance.

"It wasn't charity, unless you call worrying about family charity." Loosened of its ties around her waist, the apron was still hanging around her neck. Very gently, his eyes on hers, Max began to remove the remaining tie around her neck.

Mesmerized, Lily couldn't drag her eyes from his. Her breath stilled in her lungs. And then, as if someone had snapped their fingers and made her come to, she grabbed the apron away from him and held it against her chest as if he'd just stripped her naked.

"I'm not finished."

"Isaac here can finish up for you." He looked at the man, an ex-miner who cooked like one. "Can't you, Isaac?"

The man nodded.

Lily twisted her head around to see that Isaac had mysteriously materialized again, just as mysteriously as he had disappeared a few minutes ago. Exasperated, she waved a hand at the small man. Telling him to watch her sauce was like giving matches to an adolescent pyromaniac and asking him to tend the home fires.

"How can he finish up?" she demanded, her hands on her hips. "The man said he doesn't even know what cayenne pepper is."

"The people out there—" he jerked his thumb in the direction of the saloon "—didn't come to renew their acquaintance with cayenne pepper, they came to make your acquaintance."

She dug in stubbornly, saying black just because he was saying white. "They met me at Alison's wedding."

"All right then, they came to renew their acquaintance with you." He looked at her pointedly, the barest hint of a smile on his rugged face. Or maybe she was just imagining it. "Don't make me use my gun, Lily. Things could get ugly then."

She looked at him, stunned. Taking her hand in his, he began to pull her out of the kitchen.

"No, wait," she protested. "I look awful."

The half smile turned into a grin as he tucked a stray strand of her hair behind her ear, then pretended to survey his handiwork. And her.

"Awful never looked so good."

Lily wanted to protest again, to pull back, but she found herself being ushered out instead, unable to impede his progress in any way. It was as if she was a pull toy and he held the string.

She walked out of the cocooning heat of the kitchen into the smoky saloon, instantly engulfed in a cylinder of noise that came at her from all directions.

At first, it was hard making sense of any of it, but slowly, voices began to emerge, fragments of conversations floated by her. If not for the smoke, it wasn't all that different, she supposed, from the dining area in her restaurant.

Except that she wasn't in control here.

The instant the door closed behind her, sealing her into this place of dark mahogany, polished wooden floors and mingling bodies, she heard a piercing whistle behind her.

She closed her eyes, knowing that the sound had come from Max and that he was calling for everyone's attention. Opening her eyes again, she forced a smile to her lips, wanting nothing more than to retreat back into the kitchen.

She felt Max's hands on her shoulders, propelling her forward. She felt like a prize steer at the county fair, or whatever it was they did out here for entertainment.

"Listen up everyone, this is Alison and Jimmy's sister, Lily. She's been working her tail off in the kitchen just for you. For once, you're going to have something to eat here other than dried-out beef."

"What's wrong with dried-out beef?" one of the people at the bar wanted to know. "I like jerky."

"You look like jerky," someone else hooted, and a wall of laughter went up.

"Doesn't take much to amuse them, does it?" Lily whispered to Max.

Her warm breath on his skin made his stomach contract for a moment. He disregarded it as he leaned forward so that she could hear him.

"There's that tone again," he chided. Her profile was toward him and he saw her purse her lips in what he took to be a petulant expression. He bet she could throw tantrums with the best of them. "Try smiling for a change. They're not a bad lot when you get to know them. Most folks around here are willing to meet you more than halfway."

She turned around to face him squarely. "Maybe I don't want to make the trip."

Max figured he'd done all he could for now. Sometimes, it was better just to retreat than to hang around and get yourself chewed up.

"Then, lady," he told her, turning on his heel, "it's your loss."

She hadn't expected him to walk away just like that. She'd expected him to try to convince her. Perturbed, Lily stared after his retreating back even as it was being swallowed up within the crowd.

"Hey, Lily, what's your pleasure?" Ike LeBlanc called out to her from behind the bar he still enjoyed manning on occasion.

She could still make out a little of Max's departing back. Her real pleasure would be pounding on it. With effort, she roused herself, wondering what it was about that man that brought out the worst in her.

Smiling again, she turned toward Ike. ''Wine,'' she said. ''White.''

''White wine it is, darlin'.'' Ike reached behind the counter for a bottle of his best.

As he poured her a glass, he smiled to himself. Aside from being an entrepreneur, he read people for a living. He could read Lily Quintano with little effort and he'd had Max's number for a while now. This looked like it had the makings of a rather stimulating tale.

Chapter Five

Lily had been trying to work her way back to the kitchen for the last fifteen minutes, but every time she found an opportunity, someone would start talking to her.

She had to admit that this was an incredibly friendly place. The people here were more gregarious and colorful than the regulars who frequented her restaurant.

At the moment, she was talking to Max's grandmother, Ursula, who, at seventy-two, seemed to possess more energy than she did. More accurately put, Ursula was talking to her. The older woman was extolling the virtues of living in Hades. Or maybe she was talking about Max, Lily wasn't sure.

In either case, she really wasn't all that interested.

Max had been swallowed up by the crowd. The only time she'd seen him this past hour he was with a rather nubile-looking blonde, barely out of high school, who was hanging on his arm and his every word.

Probably did a lot to feed his ego. Well, if he was that shallow, she was glad he'd walked away when he had. She was through with shallow men.

Through with men entirely, she reminded herself.

The commotion coming from the direction of the kitchen caught Lily's attention. Turning, all she could see was that the door was open. The next moment, she heard Ike's voice.

"Careful, hot stuff, coming through. Hot stuff. Don't mean you, little darlin'" he said, winking at her.

Lily realized that she was directly in the way of the tables that had been placed end to end against the far wall. Ike was carrying one long, rectangular pan filled to the brim with the spareribs she'd made. He looked as if the pot holders he was using were beginning to allow the heat to come through to his hands.

"Back off, barbarians, until Luc and I set these pans down." His booming voice rose above the din. He sidled by her. "I'd step out of the way if I were you, darlin' or they'll wind up taking a bite out of you in their feeding frenzy."

Lily moved as far back as she could from the main source of activity. She realized that she was smiling. Again.

Contrary to all her expectations, the evening had

gone fairly pleasantly. The only other time she'd been here, it was for Alison's wedding and then Allen had monopolized her to the exclusion of almost everyone else. He'd spent most of the two days they stayed in Hades pointing out everyone else's foibles and looking down his nose at their lifestyle.

She hadn't thought very much about it at the time, but now she realized that at least some of his opinions had tainted her own.

She knew better, damn it. What had she been thinking?

Unlike Allen, her own roots had been on the humble side. If not for a few good breaks and a selfless older brother, not to mention the strong, supportive family network the four of them maintained, who knew how she would have wound up? Who was to say that she wouldn't have been on the far side of poor, struggling to make ends meet, satisfied with little, the way she knew at least some of these people had to be?

She wrapped her fingers around the almost-empty glass of wine she was still holding. Now that she thought of it, she *was* satisfied with little. She had no extravagances, no long-range goals other than improving the restaurant. Her closet wasn't teeming with expensive clothes and there was no jewelry overflowing the small jewelry box on her bureau, just a few choice pieces left to her by her mother.

And an engagement ring that she intended to sell the first chance she got.

There was no Mercedes in her garage, nor was her

address an exclusive one in the trendiest section of Seattle, just fairly upscale.

She did, however, have to admit that she enjoyed being a success and *Lily's* had given her that. It felt good to succeed at something, she thought, lifting the glass to her lips and taking one last sip.

The pans deposited on the tables, Ike and Luc no sooner stepped back than the locals who filled the Salty swarmed around the food.

"Wow, look at them. You'd think they hadn't eaten in days," Ike marveled.

Plates and napkins had been forsaken in a bid to score more of the ribs before they were gone. Everyone was trying to get their share.

Lily smiled. Watching what amounted to a silent tribute did her heart good. Nothing like approval, she thought. At least she knew how to do this, how to set a person's taste buds on end so that they almost sat up and begged.

"Maybe it has something to do with the way it tastes and not their starvation level," she suggested to Ike.

Ike laughed good-naturedly at the correction. "Only one way to find out."

Elbowing his way into the fray, Ike plucked one rib out for himself. It took more doing than he anticipated. Having won his piece, he took a bite. The easygoing grin on his face changed to a look of amazement. He ate slowly, savoring, experiencing. When the rib was picked clean, he looked at Lily, genuine respect and admiration in his eyes.

"Darlin', if I wasn't already a happily married man, I'd drop down on one knee and beg for your hand—as long as the other hand was stirring a pot of this sauce." He looked at the denuded piece in his hand, his mouth watering for another. "What *is* it?"

"Exclusive," Lily replied, her eyes dancing. While she had expected the taste to knock his socks off, she hadn't known whether or not the man would be willing to admit it. She liked his openness.

Pretending to sidle up to her, Ike raised and lowered his brows like a villain from an old-fashioned melodrama. "I couldn't perhaps talk you into parting with the recipe, could I?"

Tickled, Lily laughed and shook her head. "No."

"It's something she came up with after a lot of trial and error," Jimmy volunteered, coming up beside her. "Lily'd sooner part with a kidney than tell you what she puts into her barbecue sauce."

Isaac materialized not too far from the discussion they were having. "It's got cayenne pepper in it," he offered.

Ike nodded. "That's a start."

Lily turned in the little man's direction. "Not nearly enough cayenne pepper right now," she reminded him.

He gave her a contrite, sorrowful look.

She suddenly felt guilty about her earlier testiness. She supposed her mood could be attributed to a whole combination of things. Less than an hour ago, her self-esteem had been in tatters. After all, it was difficult to come to terms with the fact that she'd spent her affection on the wrong man. What was more, she'd come to the painful realization that there probably wasn't a right man out there, at least, not for her.

She knew she wasn't the easiest woman to live with and if the tables were turned, she probably wouldn't have wanted to put up with a male version of herself. But all the same, she was who she was and at least her heart was in the right place when it came to her family and handful of friends.

Just not when it came to romance.

Perhaps she could blame her change of heart on the wine, or the fact that there was little to no air in the place, or that her efforts were being so wholeheartedly appreciated. Whatever the reason, she was feeling magnanimous. And that meant an apology was in order.

"I'm sorry, Isaac," she said, surprising those around her who knew and loved Lily. "I didn't mean to snap at you earlier. It's just that—"

"She gets surly in the kitchen if everything isn't going right," Alison confided to the bewildered little man.

"Not surly," Lily objected. Couldn't her sister use a more flattering, compassionate word?

"Surly," Max attested, coming up behind her.

The sound of his voice caught her off guard and Lily turned suddenly, surprised at how close he was. She knocked against his hand. The hand that was holding the remainder of the sparerib he'd gotten for himself. Apparently, whatever their differences were, they didn't prevent him from eating what she'd made.

There was a mess on his chest where the sparerib had blotted itself. Embarrassed, Lily tried to make light of the situation and her clumsiness—which wouldn't have happened if the man hadn't snuck up on her like that. "I guess that sparerib sauce doesn't go all that well with a sheriff's badge, does it?"

He shrugged, looking down at the splotch of rust-colored sauce on his chest and badge. "I dunno, maybe you've found a new way to polish it. People use toothpaste on jewelry."

Finishing off the last bit of meat from the bone, Max reached around her and placed it on the plate set aside to collect the remains. He took out his hand-kerchief and wiped his fingers and his lips.

Lily tried not to watch his every move, not really knowing why she was doing it in the first place. "I wouldn't know. I don't spend time cleaning jewelry."

He'd already noticed that except for a small gold cross and the hoops that swayed at her ears with every move she made, Lily wasn't wearing any jewelry. The big, gaudy diamond that had resided on her left ring finger the last time she'd been here was gone.

"How about hair?" he asked.

Perfectly arched brows came together in confusion. The other people in the wide saloon faded away for her. "What?"

He nodded at the back of her head. "You've got some of the sauce in your hair."

Eyes widening in surprise and horror, Lily reached behind her to see if Max was putting her on. He wasn't. Her hand came in contact with something messy.

"Oh." She wrinkled her nose. Now what?

"C'mon," he volunteered, "you can clean that off in the kitchen." He glanced up toward the swinging door. It looked like a good part of the crowd had shifted there in hopes of more food emerging from the ovens. He shook his head. He'd never seen the miners behave this way. But then, he had to admit she made a hell of a mean sauce. "If you can get near it," he qualified, doubtful that she could. "Looks like the vultures are circling the area, scavenging for seconds."

"I used all the ribs you had," she told Ike. If he'd placed them all in the pans, then they were out of luck.

It was clear that he'd made a mistake in his order. "There are usually a lot of leftovers," Ike told her. "But then, I guess this crowd has never sampled your sauce before."

Max saw her beaming at the compliment. Taking her empty wineglass, he placed it next to the plate filled with bones and took her hand. Closing his fingers around it, he began to thread his way to the side of the saloon. Once there, he started to lead her up a staircase she hadn't even noticed.

"Where are you taking me?" she shouted so that he could hear.

He didn't feel like shouting, so he made no answer. At the top of the stairs, Max veered to the left and opened a door for her.

"Ike and Luc used to live here before they married Marta and Alison and moved into houses of their own. They still keep this open for any of the locals who have a little too much to drink and can't drive home."

She thought of the wide, empty space surrounding the Salty. It wasn't as if anyone driving slightly inebriated was likely to incur even moderate traffic, or another vehicle for that matter.

"What could they possibly hit?"

Spoken like a woman from the big city. "You'd be surprised." He gave her only a few particulars. "Jake Zoltif ran into a moose. Pete Carney drove his car right into a snow drift, got out and started wandering around. It took us almost two days to find him. Lucky it was early May or he might have froze to death. Ike and Luc feel better if their patrons don't run the risk of hurting themselves or the wildlife, so they maintain beds up here."

She looked into the small room with its three beds all made up and no one in them. Something quickened within her.

Had he brought her up here to seduce her?

Lily tried to pull her hand away. "I don't need a bed."

"No, no one said you did. But you could use some water and they've got a bathroom up here," he replied, unfazed by her implication. He opened the door to the tiny facility and gestured toward it. "It's not exactly the latest thing, but the water runs and the toilet flushes, sometimes even at the same time," he added with a grin.

Embarrassed by what she'd been thinking, she avoided his eyes and muttered, "Thank you," as she passed him and went in.

Holding her hair up over her head, Lily looked in the mirror, trying to locate the offending glob of sauce.

Shaking his head, Max came to her rescue. "You're not going to see it that way. It's right here." He touched the spot that was against the nape of her neck. "Here, I'll get it for you," he volunteered, knowing that she'd either need eyes in the back of her head or another mirror to see it properly. As far as he could tell, she had neither.

Turning on the water, Max took the washcloth from the tiny towel rack on the side of the sink and held a corner of it under the faucet. Satisfied that it was wet enough, he started to wipe the discolored area of her hair.

Self-conscious, Lily tried to reach for the cloth. "I can—"

"Hold still," he chided. "I've got two sisters, one on either side of me. I know what I'm doing."

The strokes were slow, sure. Soft, when she'd expected him to be heavy-handed, like a bear pawing at a cache of just-discovered honey.

Lily was surprised that he could be so gentle. He didn't seem the type. Raising her eyes, she studied his face in the mirror. Max looked completely absorbed in what he was doing.

Something stirred inside her and she banked it down, knowing it had happened only because of her vulnerability.

Seeing Alison with her husband and Jimmy with his wife had created an ache within her, a cry that echoed, *Why not me, too?* But that was brought on just by the moment. She already knew the answer. She wasn't like them, and her needs were different. Most of all, she didn't want a man she could over-power, overrule. But anyone who would stand up to her would try to put her in her place and she didn't want that, either.

Damned if you do, damned if you don't, she thought with a touch of sadness.

She was destined to live and die as exactly as what she was, a workaholic.

At least she had a family she could lavish attention on, she consoled herself.

She continued to watch Max work. Who would have thought that hands that large, that strong, could be so gentle? "Your sisters get sauce in their hair often?"

He raised his eyes and met hers in the mirror. For a second, he stopped cleaning. And then his pulse started again and he pretended not to notice that look-ing into her eyes had taken his breath away.

"Not sauce," he corrected, "gum." He remem-bered several incidents and the time that his grand-mother had actually used soap to wash out June's mouth. He still didn't know where she, at eight years old, had picked up that kind of language. It had been an unspoken town rule that miners never swore around children.

"Gum?"

"June is—was," he amended, although he wasn't altogether sure the term he was about to use didn't still apply to his sister, seeing as how she wore motor oil as easily as some girls wore cologne, "a tomboy. She got gum stuck in her hair more than once." And screamed blue murder when he worked to get it out. He had more patience with June than April did. Probably because he thought of her as a little doll while April had her pegged for what she was, a holy terror.

Okay, she'd play along with this homey scenario for argument's sake. "How did you—"

"I used peanut butter," he said matter-of-factly.

That impressed her. She thought of her own big brother, knowing how lost she would have been without Kevin and how much she and the others loved him. Maybe this frontier sheriff on an ice floe really wasn't such a barbarian, after all.

"There," he announced, putting the washcloth down on the rim of the sink. "You're sauceless again." Max peered at his handiwork. "Basically," he added under his breath.

Lily turned around to face him. The small, pedestal sink was at her back, eating up most of the closet-like space.

This was too close for comfort. Her mouth felt drier than it should have. Other parts weren't dry at all. Such as the palms of her hands. Unconsciously, she rubbed her fingers along them.

"Thank you," she murmured, doing her best to sound authoritative.

The small words had him smiling at her. "There, that wasn't so hard, was it?"

She was instantly on the defensive. She liked it better that way. Her chin rose in a silent challenge. "Am I being chided again?"

God, but she took offense fast. "Funny, I thought it was a compliment."

"'Compliment'?" she echoed incredulously. "How was that a compliment?"

Max blew out a breath. "Okay, wrong word. Comment, then. Observation," he added in case the second word didn't suit her fancy, either. "Do you always like to argue?"

There he was, criticizing her again. She stood her ground. "No, do you?"

He would never have realized that his patience was limited if it hadn't been for her. "Lady, until you came into my life, I never argued at all."

Her hands went to her waist automatically, her eyes darkening. "Are you saying that I bring out the worst in you?"

She was putting words into his mouth. "Did I say that?"

Damn it, why couldn't he just admit she was right, apologize and back off? "No, but you implied it."

His temper threatened to flare. "If I implied it, I would have known."

Because he was a relative stranger, not to mention technically a relative, she bit back a few choice words she would have hurled at him under other circumstances. But she couldn't hold back what she thought of him.

"You are the most annoying man I have ever encountered."

A calmness set in and he held on to it. "I don't see how that's possible," he informed her coldly. "I've met your fiancé."

She could feel her temper escalating. She didn't need this aggravation. She should have never let him drag her out of the kitchen.

"Ex-fiancé," she corrected. "And keep Allen out of it."

"Why?" He wanted to know. "Because you still have feelings for him?" And why that question had suddenly risen to his lips was a mystery he didn't think he'd be solving in the near future. What the hell had come over him?

"No, because you're sitting on your high horse, criticizing my choice, and it's none of your damn business who I chose."

He looked at her mildly, cutting her dead. "Never said it was."

For a second he'd taken the wind out of her sails. Feeling cheated, she decided to shout at him anyway. "Damn straight it's not. Now if you don't mind, I'd like to get out of this claustrophobic box and go back down to my family."

Seething, Lily tried to push him out of her way. She wound up brushing against him instead. The full length of her body was suddenly pressed against his as she plowed forward before he could step back.

Her mouth fell open as every inch of her body felt an overwhelming current fly through it.

Damn it, she thought, she wasn't supposed to be feeling this. Whatever the hell "this" was. Lightning. Electricity. Chemistry.

Something.

Something that started everything churning within her and caused desires to surface from where she'd thought she'd buried so far down that they could never rise up again.

Why?

Angry, confused, resentful, Lily stared up at him, dumbfounded.

She was doing it again. Looking up at him with those wide eyes of hers. Changing the temperature of his blood from normal to overly warm. He could feel the heat rising, spreading. Finding its way to all parts of him and holding him in its grip.

He was either about to come down with something or to do something very, very stupid.

For both their sakes, he hoped he was coming down with something.

Before Max knew exactly what was happening, he found himself cupping her face with his hands. Searching her eyes for something. What, he wasn't sure.

The next minute he brought his mouth down to hers.

The moment that he did, all hope that this was a some rare form of closet fever or an equally curable disease was lost.

Chapter Six

Lily could remember, early on in her culinary career, being preoccupied and bending to open the door of an oven whose temperature had been set at five hundred degrees. The blast of heat that hit her face had completely sucked away her breath and almost overwhelmed her.

Kissing Max, *being* kissed by Max, was exactly like that, except that there was no "almost" to cling to, no roasting pan of squab to occupy her mind and force her to move beyond the paralyzing sensation that threatened her with complete meltdown.

And, being kissed by Max was also infinitely more pleasurable.

Struggling for control of her body and what was left her of mind, Lily couldn't make herself pull away, didn't *want* to make herself pull away.

Like a small metal filing irresistibly drawn to the surface of a giant magnet, Lily found herself wrapping her arms around Max's neck, wrapping herself around the kiss, and utterly losing herself in what was happening, withdrawing from the real world for a blink of an eye.

For an eternity.

Pleasure and a host of delicious sensations curled upward from her toes, stretched and reached out to all parts of her.

A ringing noise drifted in from a distance, growing more urgent.

With a sigh that was half annoyance, half relief, Max pulled his head away.

Pulled his lips away.

Her eyes opened and she looked up at him, dazed, disoriented.

Max curbed the desire to thread his fingers through her hair, to cup her cheek, both of which would have displayed far more affection than the kiss, which had been based on pure passion. Affection went deeper and was, he told himself, to be reserved for something more important than grappling with a sucker punch to the gut.

Still, he couldn't help smiling just a little. She looked as confused as he felt. "Either we've just discovered something very unique here and your jeans are ringing, or that's your cell phone."

Why were only half the words he was saying penetrating? She could see his lips moving. Was it so god-awful hot in this bathroom that it had affected her hearing somehow?

"What—" And then his words replayed themselves in her numbed brain, finally making sense. "Oh, right, my phone."

Flustered and annoyed at being undone this way when he looked as cool as a night in November, Lily brought her hands down from around his neck and took a step back. Reaching for the phone, which continued its demanding whine, she discovered that getting it out was a challenge she hadn't anticipated. The small black object fit snugly into her pocket. Too snugly.

Her hair fell into her eyes as she finally managed to retrieve it. Doing her best to completely ignore the amused smile on Max's face, she turned her back on him as she demanded, "Hello?"

"Lily?" It was Arthur. No one else sounded that nasal when he said her name. "I can't find the reservations book and there's a party of twelve that insists it has a reservation for tonight. You didn't make one, did you?"

She closed her eyes, trying desperately to get her bearings, both cursing and blessing Arthur's insecurities, which had come to her rescue. One more second and she might have been reduced to a pile of ashes.

That sort of thing, she promised herself, was *not* going to happen again. She wasn't going to let herself be tempted by sensations like that, although she had to admit, sneaking a side glance at Max, Allen had *never* rocked her world like that. No one had.

She struggled to get her mind back on Arthur and his question. "Are you talking about the Wannamakers?" She visualized the page in the reservations book with today's date.

"Yes." She could almost hear Arthur's less than majestic chest collapsing. "Then they did make a reservation for tonight? They've really got one?"

"They did and they do." It took her a moment to summon the information from her memory banks. Quickly, she told Arthur the menu she recalled being specifically requested and before Arthur could launch into plaintive wailing that he couldn't possibly provide it, she headed him off at the pass and told him how he could.

"Now do it," she instructed forcefully, refraining from making the command so strong as to have him fall apart on her.

Saying goodbye, she flipped the phone closed and began the task of fitting it back into the pocket where she'd gotten it.

Max made no secret of watching her struggle to return the cell phone to its place. "You know," Max said, "you might give some serious thought to chucking that thing somewhere while you're here."

With one last shove, Lily pushed the phone into her pocket. "Why would I want to do that?" she all but growled. She hated being told what to do.

He was in no hurry to return her to the party. He rather liked having a monopoly on her. The woman was certainly easy on the eye, if not the ear. But then, he thought, no one was perfect.

"I thought the point of your being here was to relax."

"It is." Maybe he could sit back all day and twiddle his thumbs, but she couldn't. If the truth be known, she really wasn't sure *how* to relax. "That doesn't mean abandoning my responsibilities."

Among which, it was a safe bet, he thought, was to point out everyone else's shortcomings. "Might give that man time to build up his own backbone and confidence if you did," he pointed out.

As much as she wanted to indulge Arthur, leaving him technically in charge was as far as she was willing to carry this. "Might give him time to ruin my reputation, too."

Now she just wasn't making any sense and although he was beginning to realize that was a peculiarity with Lily, his curiosity got the better of him. "All right, I'll bite, why keep him?"

Why did she feel as if she was compelled to defend Arthur to this man every time her assistant's name came up? Why did she owe Max Yearling any kind of an explanation at all?

"Because he's not bad as a second-in-command and he takes orders without question." She thought of the one time she'd stopped by Arthur's home with some hot soup when he had been far too sick to come to work. The apartment had been Spartan. He had no hobbies, no pets, nothing. "Besides, working at the restaurant is all he has. If I let him go, he'd fall apart.''

There was a look on her face, just for a moment, that caught his attention, that intrigued him. He wasn't even sure what it was, but it had stirred him. ''So you do have a heart.''

Instantly her chin went up as she took major offense at the observation. Her eyes narrowed into combative slits.

''Yes, I do. Do you?''

He couldn't help smiling at the verbal challenge. They'd already established that fact because something had beat pretty wildly when he'd kissed her. He found himself being stirred again and even began to reach for her, his eyes holding her fast.

But the next moment he heard the sound of feet hurrying up the wooden steps that led to the living quarters.

The slightly breathless young woman with the golden-blond hair that cascaded down her slender shoulders spared one fleeting, accusing look at Lily before her mouth curved in an inviting smile as she all but engulfed Max in her gaze.

''There you are,'' the blonde declared. ''I've been looking all over for you, Max. I thought you might have left the party.''

''No, Vanessa. I'm just helping the guest of honor get barbecue sauce out of her hair,'' he explained mildly.

''Which you were responsible for putting there,'' Lily reminded him.

She could have not been there for all the attention Vanessa gave her. The young blonde was already taking hold of Max's arm and dragging him toward the landing. It was clear that "Vanessa" wanted him away from her, the sooner the better. "Everyone's looking for you, Max."

Very gently, Max disentangled himself from the young woman's grasp and directed her hand to the banister.

"Well, then let's not keep them waiting." About to descend the staircase, Max paused and glanced back over his shoulder. "Lily?"

She didn't like the way he took charge and she definitely didn't like the way her knees still felt—as if they didn't quite belong to her.

Still, she couldn't just hover here like some lost sparrow. With a toss of her head, she replied, "I'm coming," then followed him down.

The moment they reentered the saloon, Vanessa clamped her hands on Max's arm again.

"They're playing that song I like. Dance with me, Max?" She fluttered her lashes at him. "Please."

He wanted to say no, but he didn't want to crush Vanessa's fragile ego in front of so many witnesses. It wasn't all that long ago that June was this age and suffering from her first heartache. So he smiled and said, "Sure." Making certain there was a respectable distance between them, he took Vanessa into his arms and began to dance.

Out of the corner of his eye, he watched Lily melt away into the crowd.

* * *

"Your sauce was a huge success," Alison told her sister as she, Luc and Lily drove home several hours later. "As were you."

It wouldn't have taken much to be a success at that party, Lily thought. "I think a chimpanzee in a pair of jeans would have been a hit as long as she was female," she commented.

She tried to remember when she had seen so many single men gathered together in one place, and failed. They'd been friendly, too. Not the pawing, drooling sort of friendly that took place in singles' gatherings where everyone was frantic to wind up with a partner by evening's end, but the polite, warming friendly that made her feel, she had to admit, comfortable and at home. And all female.

She supposed that, in a way, the place did have its charm.

"Maybe so," Luc allowed, "but you're a great deal more appealing than any chimpanzee I've ever seen, Lily." He laughed as he drove through the silent, sleeping countryside. "I think half the single men there would have been willing to marry you on the spot—"

"That's because your cousin's cooking is for survivalists and mine appeals to the palate. It has nothing to do with me."

Luc exchanged glances with Alison, a look of wonder at this sudden modesty in his eyes. Just how badly had the incident with her former fiancé affected her? He hadn't had much of a chance to interact with his sister-in-law, but he recalled a confident, gregarious woman who wouldn't have taken anything from anyone. The woman who'd just made that self-effacing comment had been badly scalded.

"What's the deal with that girl—Vanessa something or other?" Trying to sound casual, Lily hesitated, wondering if by asking she was implying that she had anything beyond idle interest in Max. She didn't want the wrong idea to make the rounds, but then, this was Alison and Luc she was talking to and if she couldn't trust them not to spread rumors, then she might as well just give up on life entirely.

"Ulrich?" Luc asked.

She wasn't sure that was the girl's name. "The one who was following Max around," she elaborated. "Are they…together?"

"Only insofar as she dogs his tracks," Luc told her. He felt Alison press her hand on his knee, silently communicating. He knew exactly what she was thinking. He agreed. There was interest here and he wasn't about to say anything that would discourage it. "Vanessa's had a crush on Max ever since she was ten years old."

Lily wasn't exactly sure how old the young woman was, but she had a figure that undoubtedly could launch a thousand daydreams. "And he doesn't—"

"No, he doesn't," Luc was quick to assure her. "Max's not the type to pay attention to underage girls."

"Is she underage?" The girl's body certainly wasn't, she thought. The low-cut T-shirt and jeans looked as if they'd been painted on. "I thought—"

"She just turned eighteen," Luc told her. "Everyone around here thought that she'd take off, like so many of them do when they reach that age. But she's decided to hang around a little longer before she makes plans." He was repeating when Matt Ulrich had told him at the Salty less than a month ago. The man hoped that his only daughter would decide to remain permanently.

Lily shrugged, in case either of them thought that any of this mattered to her beyond making conversation. "She's very pretty."

"And very young," Luc pointed out.

"I thought you just said—"

"There's young chronologically," Alison told her. "And young emotionally. Vanessa's the latter." The girl was a schemer, a manipulator, playing young men against each other from the time she was fifteen. Someday the girl was going to cause real trouble if they weren't all careful.

"Pretty isn't the only criteria that means something, even in a place like this," Luc told her. "We get snowed in a lot in the winter and you have to be able to get along with the person you've picked to stay at your side. Otherwise," he laughed, "Max would have a rash of mysterious homicides to look into."

"Vanessa likes to play one man against another to feed her ego." Alison went on to explain how the girl's mother had died when Vanessa was little more than a child and how she, Alison, felt sorry for her, knowing what that was like. Thank God she'd had a brother like Kevin to care for her and to make sure she was raised with the right values. Matthew Ulrich, she lamented, just wanted someone to cook and clean for him while he worked.

Lily nodded, letting the discussion die. She was still fairly unconvinced that there wasn't something between Max and the young girl. The look in Vanessa's eyes when she had gazed at Max had been both adoring and possessive. The look Vanessa had directed at her had been full of poison.

Not that any of that mattered to her, Lily reminded herself. After all, in a couple of weeks she'd been back in Seattle and the people in Hades would be little more than a vague memory for her.

Lily heard the knock on her door. "I'm going to sleep in today, Aly. Don't worry about me, just go about your lives as if I wasn't here," she said from beneath her blanket.

Alison thought of protesting, but then decided that maybe Lily would be better off if she were left on her own for a while. In the five days she'd been here, she and Luc, Jimmy and April had all taken turns escorting Lily around the area. Maybe she needed some time by herself. "Okay, it's your vacation. I'll be at the clinic if you change your mind."

"I won't," Lily promised.

She listened for the sound of receding footsteps and then, throwing off the covers, breathed a sigh of relief. For the past five days, she had felt as if she were being baby-sat. They were all being very nice to her, but she felt as if she were taking them away from their lives and she didn't want that. She knew she didn't appreciate having her own life disrupted.

She was a grown woman and capable of entertaining herself.

The first thing she wanted to do was to sleep in. But the inner clock that was set to getting up early enough to make the rounds on the docks for the best fish, the choicest shellfish, refused to shut down.

After tossing and turning for almost an hour, Lily gave up and got up.

The house was so quiet, she could hear the wood creaking as the early morning sun intensified, warming the boards and drying any moisture that still clung from the night before. She showered and went downstairs to make her own breakfast.

Alison had been insisting on feeding her and, while Alison was trying hard, she still had a long way to go to be considered a good cook.

After breakfast, Lily kicked back for all of thirty-five minutes. Unable to just sit around and do nothing, she decided to do a little sight-seeing on her own. She commandeered a map and Alison's SUV, which was parked in the garage. Since Luc's was gone, she assumed that they had gone in to work together. Luc had said something about going over the General Store's books.

It pleased Lily no end that the young man Alison had nursed back from amnesia had turned out to be such an entrepreneur.

At least one of the Quintano sisters had found a good man to share her life with, she thought.

Feeling a little like a kid playing hooky from school, Lily took care to not attract any undue attention as she backed Alison's car out of the garage. She could have spared herself the worry. There was no one else around.

Driving away from the small pocket of streets that comprised the town proper, Lily decided to head for the heart of the wilderness that surrounded Hades. There was a lake that she remembered had looked invitingly peaceful to her, and she really did need a little solitude.

Armed with the map, she drove toward the lake.

She had to admit that the majesty of the Alaskan terrain was something to behold. The city girl in her felt obligated to add grudgingly, "If you liked that sort of thing."

She wasn't sure if she did. Oh, it was fine in small amounts, but as far as living here day in, day out, she knew she would probably go crazy. She liked to work, to be busy, to have life, not wildflowers, bustling around her.

As she brought the vehicle to a halt several yards from the edge of the water, she was struck by the breathtaking, picturesque beauty of it all. The mountain in the background was resplendent with trees lush with greenery. The lake was a crystal blue, reflecting the sun and filling her with a sense of peace.

To make it even better, there wasn't a single soul around to interrupt her. Not even Arthur. Taking

Max's advice—she would have died before admitting it—she'd shut off the phone before starting out.

For once in her life, she wanted to be alone with her thoughts.

Getting out of the vehicle, she made sure the brake was on. The last thing in the world she wanted was to have Alison's SUV slide into the lake. Anticipate the worst, she'd always told herself, that way anything less was a pleasant surprise.

She should have anticipated the worst with Allen, she thought, then instantly upbraided herself. No, no more thoughts of Allen. That was in her past. The only thing she wanted to do was to learn from the experience. No more romance for her.

Walking to the water's edge, she let the vibrant colors of the area fill her senses. The fragrances swirled around her head.

Feeling lazy for perhaps one of the few times in her life, she sat on the bank and just gazed at the water. The day was already getting hot. The water began to look better and better to her.

Pressing her lips together, Lily looked around. What was to stop her from going in and enjoying the water? There was no one around to see her.

In a moment of daring, she decided to do it, to indulge herself and for once do something wild and reckless. Shedding her clothes, leaving them on a nearby bush, she slipped into the water.

The cold was a surprise, but not entirely unwelcome. Within a few minutes she'd acclimated completely.

Lily swam for a little bit, taking care never to go too far or to lose sight of the bank or her clothes. The last thing she wanted to be was lost and naked.

Before long, a tranquillity found her, enveloping her slowly and seeping into her system. She supposed she could see the allure of a place such as this—to visit, not to live. The fast-paced world she usually dearly loved seemed a million miles away.

And then she heard it.

A deep rumbling noise, a little like an approaching train. Except that this was not coming from a steel-and-metal thing, this noise was coming from a bear. A large black bear not too far from her, intent on fishing for its noonday meal.

The scream escaped her lips before she could think to stop it. As she held her breath, she saw that the worst had happened. She'd drawn the bear's attention to herself.

The almost docile, lumbering creature became a two-ton threat. The fish he'd just been after was abandoned as he clambered back onto the bank and headed in her direction.

Already swimming madly for the bank, Lily soon shot out of the water and ran past the bushes where she'd left her clothes. She made a grab for the long blouse. With effort she managed to pull it on as her legs pumped madly.

Stones cut her feet. She ran into the woods, hoping she still remembered how to climb a tree, hoping she would make it up one before the bear got to her.

She could hear the animal behind her, crushing everything in its path beneath its heavy weight as it came after her. Lily ran deeper into the woods, more terrified than she had been the time she had eluded a mugger on the darkened streets of Seattle. Thanks to Kevin's insistence, she knew enough martial arts to defend herself if it came to that, as long as the mugger wasn't carrying a knife.

But a bear, there was no defending herself against a bear.

Damn it, why had she come out here? Why had she let someone like Allen scramble her thinking, undermine her self-esteem to this extent, forcing her to go somewhere to pull herself together? She should have given him his traveling papers a long time ago.

The thoughts, seemingly complex, shot through her brain in an instant as she leaped up for a branch, grabbed it and then scrambled up the tree. The bark cut into her flesh as she made her way up.

Finding a perch, Lily held on, waiting, listening. Holding her breath until the bear appeared.

But he didn't.

The shot that rang out a few minutes later had her jerking spasmodically.

And then there was nothing.

She remained where she was, not convinced that she was out of danger or that the bear was gone. These animals were much more clever than they were given credit for. She watched the Discovery channel; she knew.

Trembling, she realized that that heaviness she felt against her was the cell phone. She'd left it in her shirt pocket instead of in her jeans. Hands shaking, she reached for the phone, her pride completely gone. She was going to call Luc and ask him to come get her.

But the phone tumbled from her fingers and landed on the ground. She cursed her clumsiness and her idiocy for coming out here alone in the first place.

"Won't do you any good around here. There's no signal in the woods."

Startled, she nearly lost her hold on the branch, making a grab for it at the last moment. Her heart pounding just as hard as when she'd first seen the bear coming toward her, Lily twisted around in her perch to look down at the base of the tree. Instead of the bear, she saw Max looking up at her.

For a second she remembered hearing of legends about men who were half animal, half wolf and could change at will, materializing wherever they wished. She wasn't sure if the origin of the legend was in Native American lore, something that arose out of Irish myths, or even perhaps something Alison had passed on to her from the local Inuit tales.

All she knew was that if there was such a thing, Max Yearling would have made a perfect candidate.

She clutched at the trunk of the tree, even as she tried to keep the hem of her blouse down as low as possible. "What are you doing here?"

He forced himself to stand where he wasn't looking directly up her long blouse, although he had to admit it wasn't easy. The woman's body was pretty near perfect. "I patrol this area, remember?"

She tugged at the hem of her blouse, wishing it was longer. Wishing she had never gone for that swim and had clothes on. Wishing she was home in Seattle in her own bed. "Like a mountie."

"Like a sheriff," he clarified.

She couldn't swallow. There was no saliva in her mouth.

"And you just happened to be here," she mocked.

"Not exactly," he admitted. If he kept on talking to her like this, he was going to get a crick in his neck. "I was following you."

"Follow—following me?" she demanded, stunned. Furious. Had he been watching her this whole time? Hidden like some voyeur while she'd taken off her clothes? Had he stood there, ogling her? "Why?"

"Because I saw you take off by yourself. Not really a good thing for a tenderfoot to do around here, even in the summertime."

She frowned, knowing she should be grateful to him, unwilling to give him any credit at all. It was easier being angry. "It's not exactly my foot that's tender," she snapped. "Were you watching me the whole time?" The thought aroused heat that covered her in the form of an intensifying blush.

"The whole time," he allowed. "At a discreet distance, of course. And before you ask, I did turn away when you started peeling off your clothes."

Right. She just bet he did. For her own sake she pretended to believe him. The bark was digging into her feet and they were beginning to ache.

She looked out, but saw little except trees. "Where's the bear?"

He glanced over his shoulder just to make sure he was right. "I don't think you have to worry about him anymore."

She thought of the shot she'd heard. "Did you shoot him?"

"No. That was probably Victor."

"Victor?" She didn't remember meeting anyone by that name at the Salty.

"He's a local around here. Keeps pretty much to himself. He probably saw you and fired to scare the bear away."

That didn't exactly reassure her. "Then he's still out there? The bear, I mean."

"Nothing for you to worry about right now," he told her. Humor tugged at his lips as he saw her mentally consider her options. "Are you planning on setting up housekeeping up there?"

"Don't rush me," she snapped. "And don't look." Extending a leg, she tried to reach the next branch down. She pulled her foot back when no contact was made. Somehow, it had been a lot easier to scramble up when fear was choking her than to get down with embarrassment as her only companion.

Looking up at her, Max pushed back his hat. "You know, I'm not sure how long that bear's going to be gone. You might want to think about getting down soon."

"I'm trying," she told him through gritted teeth. "But somebody went and moved the branches."

"Always easier to get up than to get down." It wasn't a consolation. "Don't worry, if you fall, I'll catch you."

That wasn't a consolation, either. "I'm—" She was afraid, she realized. Genuinely afraid. The next moment she heard rustling directly below her and stiffened. "What are you doing?"

He was coming up to help her climb down. It was either that, or wait until she fell out. "Ever hear that thing about Mohammed and the mountain?"

"Does that make me the mountain?"

"We'll discuss that after I get you down." He was just below her. "All right, start climbing down. I'll ease you onto this branch here. C'mon," he coaxed.

When she didn't move, he shook his head, second-guessing why she was hesitating. "Lily, you haven't got anything any other woman doesn't have and I've seen it all before, so stop being shy and let's get you out of this tree before we both get old."

"I thought you said you didn't look."

"I'm making an educated guess," he replied. "Now let's get out of here before that bear decides to come looking for you. Next time, Victor might not be around."

Faced with two evils, she picked the lesser and very slowly began to extend her leg.

Chapter Seven

Lily had never felt so compromised in her entire life. With every move she made, the edge of her blouse would ride up. This was absolutely unacceptable.

She tried to make her way the short distance to Max, tugging at the hem of her blouse almost constantly.

Watching her non-progress, Max shook his head. "You need both hands."

"I know," she growled between clenched teeth, "but then I'd fall out of the tree."

He laughed. "I mean, to hold on with while you're climbing down."

She stopped tugging and moving, fixing him with a look that would have sent a lesser man running for the hills. "And create a sideshow? I don't think so."

He let out a sigh. The woman was definitely a challenge. Thinking a minute, he came up with a possible solution. At least it was worth a try.

"Okay, hold on." Wrapping one arm around the trunk of the tree for balance, Max unnotched his belt and started pulling it through the loops.

Watching him, Lily's jaw slackened. "What the hell do you think you're doing?" she demanded.

Was he getting undressed, too? Why? Just what did the natives do around here to while away the long hours?

Ignoring the sharp edge in her voice, Max said, "Coming up with a way to hold down your dignity while you climb out of the tree." From his present position, Max could just about reach her thighs. He took aim. "Hold still."

Easier said than done. Lily felt a fresh flood of warmth shoot through her as Max encircled her thighs with his belt. His hands brushed her flesh, creating havoc within her.

This shouldn't be happening, she told herself. And she shouldn't be reacting this way.

But she was and there didn't seem to be much she could do to block out the feeling.

As Max worked to cinch the belt, Lily held her breath, waiting for him to do something that she could hit him for—not entirely sure she would if the occasion arose.

He looked up at her, taking care to keep his eyes on her face and not on her hips or thighs as he slipped the metal catch through the last hole in his belt, although it wasn't as easy as he made it look. He was more than a little aroused.

Finished, he finally removed his hands.

"All right, I've got it just tight enough to keep your blouse from rising up to your waist. You can still move your legs." Seeing as how she wasn't about to make any great leaps, he didn't think that her slightly limited movement would be a problem. "Now we're going to get down inch by inch," he instructed. "Just follow my lead. I won't let you fall."

It was a promise, said without fanfare, without emotion. It was a given.

And she believed him.

Very carefully, Lily did as he told her, cautiously making her way down, acutely aware that Max's hands were hovering just around her legs, ready to steady her if the need arose.

They worked it slowly, with Max descending a foot at a time and then waiting until Lily joined him. Each time she made it down a little farther, she was vividly aware of her body sliding against his. Vividly aware of the way she felt at the moment of contact. At the promise of contact.

"Almost there," Max told her, his voice unusually gruff as she once again reached his level, her body all but fitting into his.

It was at times such as this that he found it difficult to think like a law-enforcement agent and not a man. There was just so much teasing a man could take, even if it was completely unintentional.

Not trusting himself to look anywhere else, his eyes held hers. "Ready?"

"Yes," she whispered, although she wasn't altogether certain if she meant that she was ready to go the final distance, or if she meant that she was ready for something else entirely.

The bear, the danger that had sent her up to heights she'd never even considered before, was momentarily all forgotten as she stared into the greenest eyes she'd ever seen, felt her pulse accelerating to a rate she'd never achieved without benefit of breath-stealing aerobics.

It occurred to her in that flash of an eternal second that what she might really be ready for, what she might really need, was a fling. A toe-curling, teeth-rattling, mind-blowing, body-numbing, no-holds-barred fling. And this backwoodsman with a badge might just be the one to give it to her.

No, there was no "might" about it. She was certain of it. What she wasn't certain of was how she'd handle it once she was in the middle of it.

On paper, she knew exactly how she should handle it. As though it was just one of those things. A vacation of the spirit, with no strings, no regrets and no payments when the end finally came.

But in reality, she didn't know if that was possible.

What she did know was that there was something going on here between her and the Lawman. Temporary to be sure, but very, very exciting.

She had to be crazy, thinking this way.

And yet...

Max let go of her waist, although he really didn't want to. It was nice having a reason to hold her. He was coming to her rescue, so she couldn't take him to task...too much.

But they were almost there and the ground was waiting for them just below.

He looked down, judging the distance. Couldn't be more than six feet. He turned back to look at Lily. There was fear in her eyes, even though she tried to hide it.

"All right, I'll jump down out of the tree first, then you."

Lily pressed her lips together and nodded nervously. "All right." Lily took a deep breath, as if bracing herself for him. "Go ahead."

She watched as Max positioned himself and then leaped. Like a nimble panther. Sleek, sure. Why not? she thought grudgingly. He probably spent half his life swinging from one tree or another.

Standing at the base of the tree, Max raised his arms and stretched his hands out toward her. "Nothing to it. Your turn."

"Okay." She crouched first, then straightened again, judging her chances, unable to get a good feeling about either position as a springboard.

Max waited patiently as she repositioned herself several more times. He knew that the longer she took, the worse it was for her. "Like they say in the sports ad, just do it."

About to jump, Lily stopped and looked at him in surprise. "You get commercials up here?"

"Yup." He scratched his head in an exaggerated motion. "And we been getting them-there talking pictures in the the-ater now for almost a year," he drawled.

She flushed. She supposed she had that coming. It was just that everything looked so rustic, so uncomplicated around Hades, it was hard thinking of the twenty-first century actually existing up here. "Sorry, didn't mean to insult you."

He laughed the thought away. "Take more than that to do it. I've got a thick skin."

It hadn't felt thick to her. Not to the touch, at any rate. Lily pressed her lips together, telling herself that now wasn't the time to think about the feel of his skin or the fact that his anatomy felt hard and taut each time hers slid against it. If she was distracted, she might wind up breaking her neck.

Taking a deep breath, she announced, "Okay, I'm coming down."

"I can hardly wait," he cracked.

Annoyed, she bent to try to reach his hands. Her foot slipped out from under her and she lost her balance. A high-pitched scream accompanied her descent as Lily found herself falling out of the tree and directly on top of Max. Losing his own balance, Max fell backwards.

He landed on the grass, she landed on him. Lily had the softer landing. Aching, Max still thought he got the better of the deal.

Trying to catch her breath, her hair hanging in her face, Lily jerked her head up. The rest of her re-

mained where it was. Sealed against him. Electricity
shot tingling tendrils all through her.

"I thought you said you'd catch me," she accused
hoarsely.

"I did." He grinned, trying not to laugh at the picture he knew they must have made. "I just didn't
happen to mention what position I'd be doing the
catching in." Without giving it any thought, he closed
his arms around her, holding her steady. "You all
right?"

She nodded, still trying to fill her lungs with air.

The laugh faded and the grin slowly receded from
his lips. Max was aware of the way her breasts felt
against his chest as she struggled for air. Was aware
of the way his own body reacted to the feel of her
lying like this on top of him.

If he didn't make her move, he knew there was
going to be hell to pay. A man only had so much
restraint allotted to him and then his supply ran out.
His had become painfully low.

His eyes caressed her even as he kept his hands
still. "Ready to get up?"

Why did she suddenly feel so dizzy, so disoriented?
"Yes."

Looking at one another, neither of them made the
first move.

And then he did.

Threading his fingers through Lily's hair, framing
her head with his hands, Max raised his head from
the ground just enough to brush his lips against hers.

Needs exploded within Lily, including the need to

regain the confidence she had lost. Allen's infidelity had made her feel undesirable, less than a woman. It was that feeling she was running from by coming up here. That feeling she was trying to bury.

Like a woman on fire, Lily took the lead, deepening the kiss that he'd begun into something vast and endless and all-consuming.

She heard him groan, felt him become rock-hard beneath her. Felt his hands roam the length of her body as she kissed him over and over again. The fire within her grew completely out of control, enveloping her.

He wanted her.

Wanted her to the point that he was almost mindless. Max knew that was far from good. He's always had control over himself. Always knew exactly what he was doing as he was doing it.

This sensation, this woman who had come into his life with the suddenness of a thunderbolt, had him tottering on the edge of an abyss that threatened to take all control, all thought, away from him.

Her Ice Princess pose had completely melted against him. Her movements were edgy, urgent, frantic, as if she were driven beyond desire. Driven by something that had possessed her as much as this hunger had taken possession of him.

The thought suddenly occurred to him that she was going to regret what she was doing here with him at this moment.

Regret it badly the instant it was over.

She wasn't making love to him, Max realized. It

didn't have to be him. He could have been anyone. She was making love with someone to spite the man who had hurt her. This was phantom payback.

He couldn't let her do that to herself. Couldn't let her use him that way to get back at someone who had never really counted.

It was incredibly difficult, but with the last ounce of his self-control, Max caught her shoulders and pushed her back, away from him. "I think you should get dressed."

Stunned, Lily stared at the man she had been so willing to make love with.

He was rejecting her.

After giving her every sign that he was interested in her, after all but seducing her with his looks, his kiss, he was rejecting her.

Hurt beyond belief, her dignity completely in tatters, Lily scrambled to her feet. The moment she was upright, she ran. She wasn't sure just where she was heading, hopefully to the SUV, but at all costs, it had to be away from him.

"Lily!"

Max was on his feet and chasing after her in an instant.

"Lily, damn it, you'll get lost! Stop!"

Shouting after her did nothing. She didn't even hesitate or attempt to look back. Catching up to the woman wasn't as easy as he'd thought it would be. She was faster than he'd given her credit for. Lengthening his stride even more and giving it his all, he finally managed to overtake her.

Grabbing Lily by the waist, he almost succeeded in bringing both of them down. But at the last moment he caught himself and remained upright.

Breathing hard, he held on to her tightly as she squirmed. What the hell was wrong with her?

"Why are you running away? Damn it, woman, did you forget? There's a bear still out there. And I'm betting that he's probably not alone."

"I don't care," she shouted. "I'd rather take my chances with the bear." Yanking, Lily tried to pull free, but his grip was just too tight for her. Her eyes narrowed into dagger-like slits as she twisted around to look at him. "What? You change your mind?"

He knew what she was saying.

"No," he said, his voice lowering, his eyes on hers. Desire beat a heavy tattoo in his chest. "I haven't changed my mind."

He hadn't changed his mind. He still didn't want her, Lily thought angrily. Here she was, all over him, throwing herself at him, and he didn't want her. How insulting was that? She didn't know whether to cry or to hit him. She opted for the latter.

He let her do it once. The impact of all five fingers stung his flesh, going beyond the imprint left behind. But as she raised her hand in frustration again, Max caught her by the wrist.

"The first one was free," he told her. "I figured you had to get that out of your system. But that's it. No seconds, Lily. I'm nobody's punching bag. I didn't do this to you."

Enraged, she hardly heard his protest. Was he telling her now that he hadn't come on to her? Hadn't gone out of his way to make her want to make love with him?

"The hell you didn't." As Max slowly released her wrist, she dropped it to her side. Rubbing it with her hand, she glared at him. "Oh, I forgot. You like them younger."

It was his turn to not be able to make sense out of what was being said. "What the hell are you talking about?"

"Vanessa." She spat the name out, not even knowing why any of this bothered her. Who cared who this man slept with? "That's her name, isn't it? That young thing that keeps following you wherever you go, drooling in your wake?"

He was well aware of Vanessa's designs on him. As aware of them as he was of the fact that he had done nothing to encourage them and that, like it or not, the girl needed to be protected from herself before she self-destructed.

Taking a chance, he appealed to the maternal side of the woman in front of him, not even sure if she even had one.

"Vanessa is going to get into a lot of trouble if she isn't careful. She doesn't know what to do with what she has and she's an accident waiting to happen."

If he believed that, he was more naive than she thought. "Oh, she knows, all right, Lawman, don't you doubt it. That girl knows exactly what she's got and how to use it." Here she was, standing in the middle of nowhere, wearing nothing more than an oversize blouse and his belt on her hips, arguing about the supposed virtue—or lack thereof—of a potential man-eater. She hadn't a clue as to what was going on here. "Your Vanessa doesn't exactly strike me as a train wreck."

"She's not my Vanessa," Max told her evenly. "Accidents take all sizes and shapes. And you're wrong, Lily Quintano. I don't like them younger."

He took a step toward her. A warning step he expected her to heed. She surprised him by standing her ground.

Or maybe she didn't surprise him, at that. Maybe he expected her to do just that.

"I like them with fire in their eyes and a go-to-hell attitude." He allowed himself just one touch of her hair. Taking a long strand, he sifted it through his fingers before dropping it again. "I like them with shining black hair and legs so long they make you want to fall to your knees and thank God you're alive."

Damn it, her heart had shifted again. Now it was in her throat, making it hard to breathe. Still, she raised her chin defiantly. Willing him to do something to prove her wrong.

"I don't believe you."

He shrugged as if it made no difference to him one way or another.

"Believe what you want." He shoved his hands into his pockets to keep from grabbing her and pulling her to him again. To keep from burying his face in her hair and getting lost in her scent and taste, the way he sorely wanted to. "But while you're at it, believe that what I don't want is for them to use me to get back at someone I don't even know, and from all indications, they'd wasted their own time knowing."

Because he'd hit far too close to home, Lily finally took that step back from him. "I don't know what you're talking about."

He indicated the lake's edge. Somehow, she'd managed to run exactly where she'd hoped to. Her clothes were still laid out on the bush where she'd left them. "Then it'll give you something to think about while you're getting dressed and going home."

Home?

"To Seattle?" Was he playing the heavy-handed sheriff and running her out of town because she'd cast aspersions on the chicklet that lusted after him? Was that his game?

"To Alison's," he corrected. And then, because looking at her standing there like that, with the sun outlining her nude body beneath the blouse, was making it hard for him to breathe, he added, "And while you're at it, think about this."

Catching hold of her shoulders again, Max pulled her to him and kissed her. Long and hard and with every bit of the pent-up energy he was trying so hard to contain and hold in check.

For her sake as well as his own.

Because the floodgates had never been opened within him. He wasn't sure he could close them again once they were opened, or even what the outcome would be if he did let himself go.

But even as he touched his lips to hers, he could feel that same pull he'd felt before, except more urgently now. He could take her right here, right now, without a second's hesitation.

Damn, but she was confusing the hell out of him.

Releasing Lily's shoulders, he forced himself to take a step back. He studied her face, not sure what he was looking for, not even vaguely certain he'd know it if he saw it.

"All right, now maybe you should get dressed before I forget every damn thing I just said to you and take you here and now—bear in the vicinity or no bear in the vicinity—because woman, you have stirred up something inside of me I've never felt stirred and I think that for both our sakes, we walk away from this right now, before we both do something that there'll be no walking away from."

She stared at him for a long moment, the feel of his lips on hers. Temptation whispered in her ear, caressed her body with urgent fingers. She clenched her hands at her sides, steeling herself.

The next moment she turned and hurried toward the bush where the rest of her clothes lay.

Chapter Eight

Biding his time, Max stood a discreet distance from the chest-high bush Lily had ducked behind a few minutes ago, taking her clothes with her. It wasn't easy pretending to be interested in the cloud formations overhead when every fiber of his being was centered on the woman behind the shrubbery.

He knew more than a handful of men who would have hooted at him for being so chivalrous, especially when the lady had all but thrown herself at him. But he'd grown up with a house full of women, his sisters, his mother and his grandmother. That kind of company put a fine point on a man's conscience when it came to the opposite sex.

Opposite sure was the word for it, he thought. He'd never run into a woman as contrary as Lily Quintano and he hoped to God he never would again. Once was enough, thank you very much.

"Here."

He looked up to see that Lily had emerged from behind the bush and was walking toward him. She was holding his belt out as if it were a dormant snake, about to wake up at any second.

"I think this is yours."

"None the worse for wear," he commented. Taking it from her, he threaded the black belt through the loops of his slacks, his eyes never leaving her. "I'll drive you back."

It took everything she had to keep a civil tongue in her head. All she wanted to do was to get away from this man. When he was around her, she didn't know if she was coming or going.

Going seemed like the logical choice.

Her sister's vehicle was just exactly where she'd left it. Mercifully, the grizzly hadn't decided to sit on it or to take out its wrath on the inanimate object.

"And do what," she wanted to know, "strap your vehicle to your back? Or does it just come when you call?"

The town paid him to keep his temper, but right about now, Max figured he was being paid way too little money for the feat. Still, he managed to ignore the sarcastic edge to her voice.

"I'll have someone bring me back later to pick up my car."

"Don't bother." Striding ahead of him, she reached Alison's vehicle quickly. Lily climbed in behind the steering wheel. "I can get back into town. I don't need to be baby-sat."

He put his hand on the wheel to keep her from going anywhere. "Nobody's talking about baby-sitting, Lily. This is unfamiliar country and even natives have been known to get lost. The last man who got lost and died of exposure lived here all of his life." He didn't add that it was at the height of a snowstorm in the middle of December. The woman was argumentative enough without giving her extra ammunition.

She shoved the key into the ignition and turned it on. "Why don't we just compromise? You lead the way and I'll follow."

Max studied her for a moment. He wasn't sure that she wasn't just perverse enough to take off on her own again if they went in separate vehicles. But he supposed that everyone deserved a chance, even headstrong females from Seattle.

His mouth curved. "I didn't think you believed in compromise."

She hated it when he looked at her that way, as if he were sizing her up. "I believe in anything that'll get me what I want, and right now I want to get back into town *with* Alison's car and *with* my dignity. Now if you don't mind, you're standing in my way." Max was standing right in front of the SUV. She looked at him expectantly. Waiting.

"Don't see anything wrong with that," he finally commented on her declaration of intent. He got out of her way, but the next moment got in on the passenger side.

Lily stared at him. "Just what do you think you're doing?"

He indicated the ridge up ahead. He'd left his Jeep on the other side of it. "Having you take me to my vehicle."

She read his mind instantly. Lily's shoulders stiffened. She left the vehicle in park. "What do you think, I'm going to run away the second your back's turned?"

His eyes met hers. He knew the smile infuriated her. He widened it. "The thought crossed my mind."

"Why would I do that?" she asked innocently. "We both want to head into Hades."

Doing his damnedest, he blocked out her nearness and the desire that throbbed within him, insisting on giving him no peace. Instead, he pointed toward the ridge again, as if silently prodding her to drive.

"Lily, I haven't the slightest idea why you do anything. It's not my business to know. It's just my business to keep you safe while you're here."

Safe.

The word echoed in her head and she almost laughed out loud. He certainly hadn't kept her very safe a few minutes ago when he'd kissed her. She felt as if she were one of those silly cartoon characters she remembered watching as a child. The ones that suddenly realized they were standing in midair with nothing under their feet, about to free-fall through space.

That was how he'd made her feel. As if she were free-falling through space and hadn't a prayer of landing on her feet.

But somehow, she had. Because here she was, sitting beside him, both of them acting as if nothing out of the ordinary had happened.

Except that it had.

She wasn't sure if she'd ever disliked any man half as much as Max. Not even Allen.

Alison had waited as patiently as she could for Lily to broach the subject. It occurred to her, as Lily went about her business in the kitchen, preparing dinner, that hell had a better chance of freezing over than Lily had of bringing up the subject of this afternoon.

Shifting on the stool where she was perched, shelling the peas that Lily had handed her—a task she knew she'd been given just to keep her occupied and out of the way—Alison looked at her sister.

"I saw you coming back with Max." Although she had to admit she thought it rather strange that the two were in separate vehicles. "Why didn't you tell me you were spending the day with him?"

Lily continued moving around her sister's kitchen, where she'd been for the past two hours, trying to channel the energy she was feeling into something productive. It was either that or take an ax to the woodpile still waiting to be chopped into kindling at the side of the shed.

She didn't trust herself with an ax in her hands right now.

Pressing her lips together, she didn't even spare Alison a look, afraid of what her sister might see in her eyes.

"I wasn't spending the day with him. We ran into each other."

"In the woods?" Alison asked incredulously. "What are the odds of that?"

With a suppressed sigh, Lily looked over her shoulder at Alison. Her sister was the picture of innocence. She wasn't being taken in for a second. "Astronomical I imagine. He followed me."

"Followed you?" Alison forgot about the peas she was supposed to be shelling and leaned closer. "Tell me more, this is getting to sound interesting."

"Not interesting," Lily retorted tersely, "just in the line of duty." She recited the reason he'd given her. "He said he saw me leaving town and thought I might get lost, so he followed me."

Alison nodded, resuming her appointed task. "That sounds like Max."

Was Alison referring to the part about his following her? "He's a stalker?"

"The word is protector, Lily my love." Alison's heart ached that Lily looked at things so harshly, so uncompromisingly. There was so much of life you missed that way. "You know, I think you've been in the big city so long, it's colored your perspective about things, Lily."

Lily placed the ladle down on the counter and turned around to look at her sister. What was she talking about? "Aly, in case you've forgotten, we're

all from the 'big city.' You, me, Jimmy, we were all
born and raised in Seattle. You make it sound like
you were born and bred here.''

Alison shrugged. She knew this was hard for Lily
to understand. She gave it a shot.

''Maybe I was.'' She saw Lily stare at her. ''In a
way. I feel at peace here, Lily. Like I belong. Like I
really make a difference. I never made a difference
back in Seattle.''

Lily abandoned what she was doing to cross to the
counter and her sister. Did she actually believe what
she was saying? ''Of course you did.''

But Alison knew better. ''Not like here. Here every
single person is important, necessary. We all depend
on one another, need one another.'' It was as if they
comprised one long, interconnected human chain. Or,
she amended, as if they were one big, extended family.

Lily shook her head. ''Sounds much too confining
to me.''

''It's all in the way you look at it.'' Alison waited.
But Lily said nothing, only turned back to the stew
she was creating. Slipping off the stool, Alison came
up behind her. ''So, how do you look at it?''

Lily reached for the carrots she'd peeled a few
minutes ago and began slicing them into quarter-inch
pieces. '''It'?''

''Him,'' Alison finally said with a touch of exasperation. Was Lily deliberately being coy? ''Max,''
she added for good measure before her sister could

GIFTS from the Heart

Play Gifts from the Heart and get 2 FREE Books and a FREE Gift!

HOW TO PLAY:

1. With a coin, carefully scratch off the gold area at the right. Then check the claim chart to see what we have for you — **2 FREE BOOKS** and a **FREE GIFT** — **ALL YOURS FREE!**

2. Send back the card and you'll receive two brand-new Silhouette Special Edition® novels. These books have a cover price of $4.50 each in the U.S. and $5.25 each in Canada, but they are yours to keep absolutely free.

3. There's no catch. You're under no obligation to buy anything. We charge nothing —**ZERO** — for your first shipment. And you don't have to make any minimum number of purchases — not even one!

4. The fact is, thousands of readers enjoy receiving books by mail from the Silhouette Reader Service™. They enjoy the convenience of home delivery... they like getting the best new novels at discount prices, **BEFORE** they're available in stores...and they love their *Heart to Heart* subscriber newsletter featuring author news, horoscopes, recipes, book reviews and much more!

5. We hope that after receiving your free books you'll want to remain a subscriber. But the choice is yours — to continue or cancel, any time at all! So why not take us up on our invitation, with no risk of any kind. You'll be glad you did!

A surprise gift FREE!

We can't tell you what it is... but we're sure you'll like it! A

FREE GIFT!

just for playing **GIFTS FROM THE HEART!**

The Silhouette Reader Service™ — Here's how it works:

If offer card is missing, write to: Silhouette Reader Service, 3010 Walden Ave., P.O. Box 1867, Buffalo NY 14240-1867

BUSINESS REPLY MAIL
FIRST-CLASS MAIL   PERMIT NO. 717-003   BUFFALO, NY

POSTAGE WILL BE PAID BY ADDRESSEE

SILHOUETTE READER SERVICE
3010 WALDEN AVE
PO BOX 1867
BUFFALO NY 14240-9952

NO POSTAGE
NECESSARY
IF MAILED
IN THE
UNITED STATES

turn her eyes innocently up at her and ask who. "How do you find Max?"

That was an easy one. Lily brought the knife down a little harder on the chopping block. "I find him insufferable."

Alison watched Lily chop for a few seconds and had her answer. She smiled to herself. "I see."

Lily looked up, alerted by something in her sister's voice.

"No, you don't 'see.'" Frowning, she put down the knife. She wanted this to be perfectly clear to Alison. "I know that tone, Alison Anne Quintano...LeBlanc," she remembered to add after a beat. "There's nothing to see beyond what I just said. Your wonderful sheriff's a self-centered, self-serving, annoying martinet who thinks he's God, or at least Wyatt Earp with a little Kit Carson thrown in."

"Kit Carson?"

"Daniel Boone, Jim Bridger, some mountain man, I don't remember their names," she said in disgust. Eighth-grade history seemed a long time ago.

Alison studied her sister intently as Lily spoke, becoming more and more convinced that something was going on, something Lily didn't want to admit. Something, perhaps, that her sister didn't even recognize might be for her own good. She began to believe that Lily was fighting an attraction to Max.

"Just what happened out there while he was 'stalking' you?" Alison asked, using the term that Lily had flung out so carelessly.

Lily picked up the chopping knife again and began mincing onions. "He saved me from a bear."

Had she still been sitting on the stool, Alison was certain she would have slid off. "He what?"

Lily shrugged, depositing the first batch of minced onions into the pot. "No big deal, I'm not even sure Max was the one who fired the shot. He said it was someone named Victor."

This was getting more confusing, not less. "Shot? What shot?"

Lily reached for more onions, debating the correct number for the pot size she was using. "The one that scared away the bear."

Flabbergasted, Alison cried, "What are you doing roaming around without—" Grabbing Lily's shoulder, she spun her around to face her. "You're not leaving town again on your own, understand?"

She was too old to have someone take that tone with her. "Stop sounding like Kevin," Lily told her sister. "You're not old enough to do that, or to order me around. You never were."

Age had nothing to do with it. It was a matter of the heart. "I'm old enough to not want you mauled by a bear and to worry about you," Alison insisted. "Now tell me what happened. I don't want sound bites," she warned before Lily got started. "I want the full six o'clock news version."

Lily's eyes met her sister's. A smile curved her mouth ever so slightly. She supposed, in a way, it was nice to have someone worry about her. She'd been independent so long, she'd forgotten what it felt like to have someone really care. She'd bitten Kevin's head off so many times in the past, he'd just given her her lead lately. Besides, since there were only the two of them left in Seattle, she knew he didn't want to antagonize her any more than he had to.

"Film at eleven."

Exasperation seized Alison. "Lily!"

Taking pity on her, Lily launched into the narrative. "I drove to the lake just to be by myself for a while." She thought it prudent to skip the part about taking off her clothes and going swimming. The fewer people who knew about that, the better. If Max said anything to anyone about it, she'd just deny it, she thought vehemently, convinced that he probably would. Men liked to brag. He'd probably embellish it, as well. "There was this brown bear trying to catch fish."

"A grizzly?"

"I guess." She shrugged as she went on working. She didn't know one bear from another, except that a polar bear was white. "I must have screamed when I saw him because the next thing I knew, he forgot about lunch and was running toward me."

Lily tried to sound nonchalant, but just the retelling of it made her heart beat faster. The whole thing felt almost surreal. As did what happened afterward. She banked down the stray feelings that were trying to break through.

"I ran into the forest and climbed the highest tree I could find. I heard a shot a couple of minutes later and then Max came up to the tree. He said someone named Victor scared the bear away.''

That sounded plausible. Alison had met the old man. He'd looked right through her.

''Victor's a local. Half Native American, half Inuit. He's kind of like a shadowy figure around here. Comes into town occasionally. Keeps to himself mostly. Max thinks he's the one freeing the animals out of Jeffords's traps.'' She stopped, replaying something Lily had just said. ''How'd you get down from the tree?''

A blush began to work its way up her neck, fast and furious. Lily hoped that if Alison saw it, she'd think it was the heat in the kitchen. She turned back to the chopping block.

''What do you mean, how did I get down?'' she asked self-consciously. ''I climbed down.''

Suspicious, Alison circled her, but Lily kept her back to her, working. ''Lily, I grew up with you. You never wanted to climb into the treehouse Dad made for us. You were afraid of heights, remember?'' And then the answer came to her. ''Did Max get you down?''

She knew she could lie, but it would probably backfire on her somehow. Besides, she didn't like lying to her family, beyond trying to convince them that she was doing fine.

''Yes.''

The pieces were beginning to come together. ''So he rescued you.''

Lily lifted a shoulder, letting it drop noncommittally. "In a manner of speaking."

Yes, there was definitely something going on here. "And what is it that you're not speaking?"

Annoyed, Lily put down the knife and turned to face her sister. "Alison, I work better alone in the kitchen."

"Since when?" Alison hooted. "There are at least four other people milling around in the kitchen at any one given time at *Lily's*. Don't give me that 'alone' garbage, you work best under pressure and in the middle of chaos." She moved closer, as if her nearness could drag the truth out of Lily. "So? What happened after he rescued you? Did he kiss you?"

"Why?" Lily demanded defensively. "Does he kiss everyone?"

Okay, she had her answer, Alison thought. "No, that's just the point."

Lily didn't remember Alison being this intrusive. It had to be living here in this nothing of a town that was responsible. "Then what makes you think he kissed me?"

Alison began clearing away the mess that was piling up in Lily's wake. "Because you're acting weird, even for you."

"Never say that to a woman wielding a knife, Aly." She raised it for emphasis, then began working again. "Yes," she finally said, knowing that Alison wasn't going to give up until she had her answer. "He kissed me."

Alison leaned over so that her face was not all that

far away from the chopping block. It was the only way to get Lily's attention. "And?"

"And," Lily said, her hand splayed across Alison's face, pushing her back the way she used to do when they were children. "He stopped." She moved the chopping block to a more inaccessible place on the counter. "End of story."

But it wasn't, Alison thought. It wasn't the end of the story, and that was just the point. Perhaps the trouble. Lily was very vulnerable right now and though she knew Max would never force himself on someone, maybe something had gone further in the woods than her sister had wanted it to.

Or, Alison suddenly realized, and this was the more likely event of the two, it hadn't gone further at all. And Lily had felt cheated. Maybe even undermined, especially after finding that Allen had turned to someone else to satisfy his appetites.

Lily could feel Alison's eyes all but boring little holes in her. With a sigh, she looked up. "Why are you looking at me like that?"

"Nothing." She knew better than to give voice to her suspicions. At least, not yet. Lily would have her head. "Just thinking."

Lily had a sinking feeling she knew exactly what Alison was thinking. God, she hoped that her sister wasn't planning on setting her up with Max. Or anyone, for that matter. She should have lied about the whole thing. Too late now.

"If it's not about setting the table, stop thinking

right now.'' Her eyes narrowed as she looked at Alison. ''That's an order.''

Alison smiled, saluting. ''Yes, ma'am.'' But she went on thinking nonetheless.

Evening had long since turned to night and there was a long day waiting for them tomorrow. Leaving Lily out on the porch, Alison and Luc said their goodnights and went upstairs to their room.

Getting into bed shortly thereafter, Luc commented again on the meal that his sister-in-law had served. ''Too bad there's no way to keep her in Hades. She could certainly make a fortune if she ever opened her own restaurant up here. The men haven't stopped asking when she's coming back to whip up another batch of barbecue sauce.''

The men who frequented the Salty were not exactly connoisseurs, but Alison appreciated the compliment on her sister's behalf.

''Who knows? Maybe she might.''

He watched his wife as she slipped in beside him. He loved watching her. Watching Alison was one of his favorite pastimes.

''Has she said anything?'' Though she'd been gracious, his impression was that Lily was just marking time until she left again.

Alison turned toward him in the bed, her eyes smiling. ''I think Lily likes Max.''

Matchmaking. He might have known. Ever since April had asked her brother to go with Sydney to pick Lily up at the airport, he knew Alison was hoping that romance would take root between the two. But he'd been around to witness the interaction between them and knew that Alison's dream was not to be.

"What was your first clue? The daggers she sends his way every time they talk, or the way she frowned when you brought up his name at dinner tonight?"

Sighing, Alison turned away and lay on her back, staring at the ceiling. "You're a man, you don't understand these things."

He wasn't crazy about being summarily dismissed. Especially by Alison. She knew better. "You're right, I'm a man and I understand them from a man's point of view."

He'd caught her attention. She turned toward him again, her body brushing his beneath the light sheet. "Which is?"

"That your sister's a very attractive woman who seems determined to keep men away from her." Although, he had to admit, it wasn't easy in a place like Hades. Men were willing to overlook a lot in exchange for a permanent bed partner and someone to talk to during the long nights. "Ever read *The Taming of the Shrew*?"

She'd read the play in high school once and hardly remembered it. But Luc's inference was unmistakable. "Are you saying Lily's a shrew?"

He raised a brow. Alison was nothing if not fair and honest. "Are you saying she's not?"

She laughed, surrendering. "Well, maybe a little. But she has a good heart."

He liked the way Alison stood up for the people

she loved. It was part of what made her so appealing to him. "Nobody ever said she didn't. But it is going to take a rare man to tame her," he pointed out. "Preferably one with an iron hide."

Alison snuggled against him, glad he saw things her way. "That would describe our local sheriff to a T, don't you think?"

Luc kissed the top of her head. He knew that all she wanted was for her sister to be happy, but he felt compelled to warn her anyway. "Alison, don't matchmake. If it's going to happen, it'll happen naturally."

She thought of what Lily had told her. And what she hadn't. "I think it already has."

Maybe he was missing something. Now that he thought of it, Alison did look like the cat that ate the canary. "And you're basing this assumption on...?"

"Max rescued Lily from a bear."

No one had said anything to him at dinner. He held her at arm's length, looking at her. "When did this happen?"

"Today," she said matter-of-factly. And then her grin gave her away. "She went off by herself in my car. Max, bless him, followed her, and when she got in over her head, he saved her." She sighed, hugging her husband. "Sounds like the perfect start to a romance to me."

He didn't want Alison getting her hopes up unnecessarily. "Except that she's leaving in little more than a week."

Her eyes danced as she looked up at him. "I wasn't supposed to stay, either, remember?"

He remembered every single minute of their courtship, especially when she didn't want to be courted. "Yeah, but then you found me irresistibly charming."

She sniffed. "Max is charming."

He pretended to be slighted. "As charming as me?"

The grin worked its way into her eyes where it became mischievous. "Well, I wouldn't know, first-hand."

"And it's going to stay that way."

She laughed, hugging him. "I love it when you talk forceful."

"I'll keep that in mind." He shifted so that he was over her. Luc began toying with the strap of her night-gown, slowly sending it down the slope of her shoulder. "Right now, though, I'd rather not talk at all."

"Oh?" she asked innocently. "And what would you rather do?"

He nipped her lower lip between his teeth, driving her crazy. "Guess."

She moved beneath him, stirring him. "I'd rather you showed me."

He slipped the other strap off her shoulders and then tugged at it beneath the sheet.

"With pleasure." Luc brought his mouth down to hers.

Chapter Nine

Ike looked up as the outer door opened, ushering the late morning light into the saloon's dim interior. If he was surprised to see Alison's sister coming in alone, he didn't show it.

He polished a small area on the already-clean counter and indicated that she should come forward and park herself there if she were so inclined.

Ike winked at her. "Well, darlin', nice to see you again. If you're looking for Luc, he's not here."

Lily, wearing a new pair of jeans she'd bought at the general store and a white tank top that did more than an admirable job of showing off her curves, remained for a moment in the doorway. She shook her head in response. "No, I'm not looking for Luc."

She wasn't sure just what had possessed her to

come to the saloon this morning instead of taking Alison up on her invitation to join her at the clinic. Maybe it was just a need to talk to someone. Someone who wasn't family, although she supposed if she looked hard enough, she'd find that all these people were somehow inter-related.

Or maybe she was just looking for a little noise to distract her. But the saloon was almost empty except for a pair of old grizzled-looking men playing darts and cursing each pass in something that sounded vaguely as though it might have been Russian.

She crossed to the bar, looking at Ike, who remained on the other side. "You should have stools," she commented.

He'd considered it when he and Luc had taken over, but decided it was a bad idea.

"No, gives the men a longer way to fall." Ike grinned at her surprised expression as he reached beneath the counter for a bottle of ginger ale. He placed the soft drink on the counter in front of her. "This way, when they've had too much, they just sink to their knees and find the floor without hurting themselves."

That was thoughtful, she supposed, in an off-beat sort of way. Lily looked at the bottle of soda. "But I didn't—"

The smile that had been known to melt many a heart widened. A glass joined the bottle on the counter. "On the house, darlin.'"

She watched him pop the top of the bottle and then fill her glass. Retiring the bottle, Ike gave the glass a slight push in her direction. Accepting it, she inclined her head in thanks. "Do you call everyone 'darlin''?"

"Only the ladies." His eyes smiled at her. "Because they are. Each and every one of them."

From anyone else, this would have been the supreme line. But for some reason, coming from Ike, it was believable. Still, the man had to be a handful. She thought of the outgoing blonde she'd met the other night. "What does your wife say?"

"Marta?" He went back to arranging the glasses on the shelf behind him. Lily could hear the affection leaping into his voice. "I've got the darlin'est wife in the world. She doesn't mind. She says she knows it's because I'm not good with names. I let her think that. So—" he turned around, wiping his hands on the towel he'd thrown on the counter "—are you sufficiently recovered from your encounter with the bear?"

Sipping her drink, Lily almost choked. She looked up at him sharply. And here she was, giving Max points for keeping his mouth shut. She should have known better. "Who told you about that?"

Her reaction mildly surprised him. She was acting suspiciously jumpy. He studied her closely as he answered her question.

"Why, Max did, of course. Seeing as how the bear doesn't talk. And even if he did, grizzlies usually don't come in here to socialize."

Because she was polite, Lily forced a weak smile to her lips in response. But she didn't feel like smiling. Not with the sick feeling taking hold in the pit of her stomach. Granted these people meant nothing to her, beyond her own kin, but she hated being the subject of ridicule.

"And just what is it that Max said?"

Definitely something there beyond what had been told. Ike knew he wouldn't get any more out of Max. Max wasn't the type to talk unnecessarily. That left the rest of the story in Lily's hands.

"Why, that you held your own," Ike said casually, wondering if she would fill in the blanks that were obviously there. "That when you saw the grizzly charging at you, you had the presence of mind to pick yourself out the tallest tree and climb it."

She waited for the other shoe to fall, the laughter to begin. There was only silence. Even the dart game had come to an abrupt stop as the two men retreated to their tankards of warm ale sitting on a small table off to the side.

Lily unconsciously wet her lips. "What else did he say?"

Ike topped off her glass, thinking that Max Yearling could be one lucky man—if he played his cards right.

"That he thinks Victor scared the grizzly off and it was lucky for both of you that the old man turned up when he did. Nasty things, grizzlies. They can separate a man from his liver with just one swipe of those big paws of theirs."

Again Lily waited for something to follow the Discovery-channel-like footnote. And again there was nothing more.

"And that's all he said?" she prodded.

"Yes." He kept his eyes on her. The light was dim, but not too dim for him to read the expression in her eyes. She was clearly surprised by the little he knew. "Why?" He kept the question on a conversational note. "What else is there?"

"Nothing," she said quickly, taking a long sip of her soda. Setting the glass down, she shrugged. "It's just that men embellish..."

Maybe that was all she was afraid of. And maybe not. "You're right there. But not all men. Not Max." Ike grinned. Max had had a few wilder moments in his youth, but he'd come around. As had they all, he thought, remembering his own adolescence. Only Luc had never strayed, never given anyone a moment's pause. Luc was one of a kind. "Straight as an arrow that one. Never knew him to bend the truth or take advantage of a situation." Even when he'd been a hellion, that had been true. Max couldn't lie. Ike figured it was a congenital thing.

Lily looked at the man on the other side of the bar, wavering. Did he know more about what had happened in the woods the other day than he was saying and was just being polite, or had Max really not said anything? Could the Lawman really be that upstanding?

The expression on his face gave nothing away, other than the fact that Ike LeBlanc enjoyed the company of women in such a way that both the women and his wife were happy.

Lily drained her glass, then watched Ike refill it. "What do you mean by 'take advantage'?"

Empty, the bottle went into the trash container beneath the counter. The one Luc had insisted they keep for recyclables.

"You must have noticed that little girl who's following Max around. Actually," he amended, "she's more than a little girl, she's become rather a fetching young thing these days." And trouble if he ever saw it, Ike added silently. But that was another story, one Alison's sister didn't need to hear. "There's many a man here who'd happily make her his wife. But she's always throwing herself in Max's path and you can just tell what's on her mind. But he acts as if she's still ten years old, still the little girl he rescued from the fire."

Taking out another bottle of ginger ale, he held it aloft, a silent question in his eyes.

She shook her head, placing her hand over the glass. If she had any more, she was going to float away. Or at least definitely need the ladies' room. If this place even had one.

"Fire?" she asked.

Ike nodded, putting the bottle away. "The one that took her mother, God rest her soul." The wilderness did strange things to people. He'd seen more than one person lose their mind out here. "It's said the woman was a little mad and set the fire herself while her husband slept, passed out at the table. Max was driving by on his way home and saw the fire. He managed to rescue Vanessa and her father, but her mother was trapped inside." His demeanor shelved the story now that Lily knew what she needed to know. Except to add, "He drinks a lot—Vanessa's father does."

What made people do that? she wondered. What made them abandon life and try to pickle their brains on a regular basis?

"Is he one of those people who sinks to his knees at the bar?"

"No, I used to cut him off before he got to that point," Ike told her without any fanfare. Owning the Salty wasn't just about making money. He had to live among these people. And he cared about them. They sought him out to act as their confessor and a certain amount of responsibility went along with that. "Man's an ugly drunk."

But Lily had caught on to something he'd said. "Used to?"

Ike wondered where all this questioning was headed. For a woman who seemed ready to pack up and leave, she was certainly curious.

"Doesn't come here anymore. Stays home to do his drinking." He didn't care to dwell on people's weaknesses, even drunks like Ulrich. "By the way, I've been wondering if you'd do me a favor, darlin'" He leaned over the counter, his eyes on hers. "The men have been asking me when you're coming back to make that sauce of yours again." He laughed. "Truth of it is, they're getting kind of ugly about it, so I thought I'd ask you. I'd be paying you, of course—" he added quickly. He wasn't a man who took charity, even when he needed it, which he didn't anymore. But there had been a time...

Lily waved away the words. She wasn't hurting for money. It was boredom that was getting to her. Boredom and random thoughts of Max that kept appearing out of nowhere, assailing her.

"No need," she told him. "I'd love to."

"Love to what?"

Startled and hating herself for appearing that way, Lily turned around to see what she already knew she would see. Max walking into the saloon. It was absolutely ridiculous, but she could feel her heart quickening at the sight of him.

What the hell was wrong with her?

Ike nodded a greeting. He stopped massaging the counter with his towel. "Kind of early for you, isn't it, Max?"

"Just making my rounds." The truth was, he was looking for her. Afraid she might have gone off again on her own.

She turned away, suddenly intrigued with her almost-empty glass of ginger ale. "That shouldn't take long," she commented.

What was it about this stuck-up woman that pushed his buttons? That rang his chimes louder than a cathedral bell on Christmas morning? All he could think about was spinning her around and crushing that haughty mouth of hers with his.

Damn, he sounded worse than that fool Jeremy Cross when he'd gotten smitten with Susan Tyler. The boy had been seventeen at the time and Susan had been his first love. He hadn't been seventeen for a hell of a long time, but he was sure acting it, Max thought in disgust.

"It's not just the town I patrol," he pointed out tersely.

"That's right," she said loftily. "Your jurisdiction takes in the forest."

"Just a hundred-mile radius," Max corrected, suddenly wishing he wasn't on duty and that it wasn't before noon. He could do with a stiff drink. Maybe two. Maybe then he could stop thinking about peeling that tank top off her shoulders and down to her waist.

He forced himself to sound official. "I didn't see Alison's SUV—"

So he'd been to the house. Almost unwillingly, a smile curled through her like smoke. Had he come by to see her? Had he come by to say something about yesterday? Or was Max just playing sheriff and throwing his weight around?

She sniffed, as if it didn't matter to her at all that he'd come by.

"That's because Alison has it today. Luc drove off earlier. Said something about wanting to stop by the Inuit village." He'd invited her to come along, but restless, she had decided to pass. She wouldn't have been good company and she liked Luc and didn't want him thinking less of her.

Max nodded. He knew all about where Luc had gone. But Luc didn't concern him right now. What did concern him was that he'd hardly had any sleep last night. And when he had managed to drop off, it was to dream about her. About feeling Lily's sleek, supple body on top of his and wanting her so badly that it tore him apart. A man can't sleep long with dreams like that. And he can't function long on no sleep. He was definitely facing a dilemma.

"Just making sure you weren't getting treed again," he told her crisply.

Ike could smell a battle coming on. Self-preservation meant keeping well out of the range of fire. Taking his towel, he backed away from the bar. "Well, if you two'll excuse me, I've got some things to tend to in the storeroom."

Max knew what the other man was up to. "No need to disappear, Ike." He put his hat back on his head. "I'm leaving."

"Wasn't disappearing," Ike protested amiably, "was working." And then he winked broadly at Lily. "Always working."

Maybe she should be leaving, too, Lily thought. She indicated the empty glass on the counter. "Thanks for the soda."

"Don't mention it." Taking the glass, he placed it in the sink beneath the counter and wiped away the slight watery ring that had been left in its wake. "And tell me when you're ready to take on my kitchen again."

Max's arrival had made her forget about that. Forget about everything, she thought ruefully. The reminder brought a smile of anticipation to her lips. "How's tomorrow night?"

Ike allowed his pleasure to come into his eyes.

"Tomorrow night's wonderful, darlin'. I'll see if I can rustle up some cayenne pepper for you by then."

"Not for me, for the sauce."

He winked. "Same thing, darlin', same thing."

Lily laughed and waved as she walked out.

Max was close behind her, trying not to get side-tracked by the way her hips swayed as she moved. Easier said than done. "You putting on another cooking exhibition?"

She wasn't sure if he was making fun of her or not. She was admittedly thin-skinned when it came to Max. "Is that what you call it?"

He walked with her, wondering where she was off to next and if he should offer her a ride somewhere. He did know that he wanted to be alone with her. To have her sitting beside him, even in his car, smelling of spices he couldn't name and wildflowers that he could.

"Well, it isn't just a regular meal," he said honestly. "You cook the way I figure angels do. It's nothing like I was raised on. But then, I'm not complaining," he was quick to add. "Grandma's specialty was food for the soul, not the stomach."

Lily stopped walking and looked at him. He was an unusual man, she had to give him that. Maybe even an enigma. He didn't brag like other men and he gave women their due. But there was something dangerous about him, dangerous to her way of life and, while she wasn't exactly sure what that danger was, she knew enough to keep clear of it.

So why did she want to be with him so badly? Why

had she even justified having a fling with him to herself? Why had she all but jumped his bones at the lake yesterday?

Lily had no answers. Only questions.

And one piece of evidence. "Ike told me what you said about yesterday." Max raised a brow, his look slightly uncertain. Had she spooked him? "That you didn't tell him what happened."

"But I did," he told her mildly. "You were out by the lake, the bear saw you and you climbed a tree to get out of his way."

She pressed her lips together impatiently. Was he trying to worm some kind of apology out of her? What was the angle here? Everyone had an angle, that much she'd learned a long time ago. "You didn't tell him what happened after."

Max's expression was unfazed. There was no hidden wink, no knowing look. "That's because nothing happened after."

She cocked her head, trying to decide, Ike's accolades notwithstanding, whether Max was on the level. "Is that the way you see it?"

The sunlight was glinting in her hair, making it lighter in places. He liked it midnight-black, but the highlights intrigued him.

"How do you see it?"

She hated having questions turned back on her. "What are you, part psychiatrist?"

He laughed, more to himself than at her question. "I'm part anything you want out here. Sheriff, psychiatrist, priest.'' He thought of Shayne's son. ''Fishing buddy. Anything and everything.''

He meant it, she realized. He wasn't just pulling her leg, he meant it. Believed every word he was saying. ''That must be some oath you took.''

He grinned at her and she could feel its punch right into her stomach. ''Does cover a lot of territory.''

Whatever comment she was to make was forgotten. The sound of screeching tires caught his attention. Max looked toward the north side of town just as a car came to a sudden, noisy halt in front of the jail across the street. He recognized it. It belonged to Sam Jeffords.

The next minute he saw Jeffords get out, open the rear door and roughly yank someone out of the vehicle. Two of Jeffords's men piled out of the other side of his car. But it was the tall, gaunt man Jeffords was manhandling who had his undivided attention.

Victor.

''Looks like I need to be covering some more,'' he said, picking up on her last comment.

Without another word, Max hurried toward the jail.

Lily didn't even stop to think her actions through, she just reacted. Following him, she practically trotted until she caught up and could fall into step beside him. For the first time since she'd met him, he looked genuinely concerned.

''What's going on?''

He didn't say anything in response, although she was certain he knew the answer.

Instead, Max called out the same question to the

men who were about to enter the jail. "What's going on, Jeffords?"

The tall, gray-haired man swung around, his hold on his captive never slackening.

"'What's going on'?" he snarled at Max, incensed. "I'll tell you what's going on. I caught him at it. You're there," he growled at Max, "twiddling your thumbs and looking the other way because you're pals with these people, but I caught him red-handed. Caught him springing my traps. Destroying them," he raged. "Now I want you to do something about it." The fact that he couldn't seem to rile Max angered him even further. "Damn it, Yearling, a man's got a right to earn a living."

Max rarely, if ever, lost his temper and now wasn't the time, even if he thought of Jeffords as the hind part of a horse. Saying so wasn't going to help Victor.

"No question about it," Max agreed easily. "And I'd say from the way you spend money that the living you're earning is a pretty good one."

Jeffords narrowed his eyes, his bushy brows touching in an angry line above them. "That's my right. I'm within the law."

Max inclined his head, remaining infuriatingly in perfect agreement with the other man. "That you are."

The other two men with Jeffords began talking, explaining how they'd caught Victor destroying one of the traps and had taken him prisoner. Max completely disregarded them. He wasn't interested in what they had to say. His main concern was Victor and resolving the situation as painlessly, as quickly, as humanly possible.

For a long moment he and Victor looked at one another, the other man meeting his gaze unwaveringly. Victor was a proud, proud man, despite the setbacks life had given him.

They'd talked about this before, when Max had gone to the man's quarters in the hills to question him about the traps. "Victor, I warned you about this. What do you have to say for yourself?"

Victor shifted his gaze and looked out at the wilderness beyond Hades's parameters. Saying nothing.

"I want him charged. I want him charged and tried," Jeffords demanded. "In the old days, he'd be hung by the neck until he was dead."

This had all the signs of getting out of hand if Max let it. "These aren't the old days, Jeffords." Max paused, thinking. "How many traps has Victor destroyed?"

"That's not the point—" Jeffords protested.

"That *is* the point," Max told him evenly.

He was like the calm center of a storm, Lily thought, wondering where Max was going with this and if these men would overwhelm him the way they clearly wanted to. The man he was defending looked as if he was completely removed from what was going on around him. It was difficult to say how old he was. His carriage was proud, his manner quietly defiant. The old man was serenely regal, she thought. As regal as the hills he inhabited.

Jeffords threw up his hands. "I don't know, ten, twenty. Hard to say."

"Say fifteen." Max looked into Jeffords's eyes. "How much did that set you back?"

With a huff, Jeffords paused to tally the amount in his head. The cost came to several hundred dollars.

Max nodded, taking the information in, his expression never changing. "Now if I was to give you that money, would you drop the charges against Victor? Call it square?"

Taken aback, Jeffords stared at him. "Why would you do that?"

"That's not the question," Max pointed out mildly. "The question is, would you call it square?"

Jeffords glared at the man he'd brought in. "He'll do it again."

"No." Max looked at Victor until the man turned and his dark eyes met his own. Max saw what he needed to. "He won't. I give you my word. Now how about it, will you drop the charges?"

To Jeffords the bottom line had always been money. "I suppose."

It was the answer Max wanted to hear. "All right. I'll come by your place later with the money."

"See that you do," Jeffords warned. Sending a few choice warning words the old man's way, Jeffords and his men grudgingly got back into the car and drove away.

Max waited until they had gone before turning toward Victor.

"Now I gave him my word, Victor. You're not the

kind to make a man break his word. I know why you're doing what you are, but you can't stand in the way of progress. Not every time, anyway. There's still plenty of ermine and beaver left. If some of them weren't caught, they'd overbreed and then starve to death because there wouldn't be enough food for all of them. You know that. It's nature's way of making sure that things continue.'' Max glanced toward the departing vehicle. "Sometimes, nature's just got an ugly face, that's all.''

There was just the faintest hint of a smile on Victor's lips. Then he inclined his head slightly, indicating his agreement to the bargain.

It was all Max needed. "Okay, you're free to go.''

But as Victor began to walk away, Lily put her hand on his sleeve. When he looked at her, she felt as if she was in the presence of something timeless and as old as the lake she'd been swimming in just yesterday.

Max looked at her in surprise, but she had to know. "Did you scare that grizzly away yesterday?''

Victor said nothing, gave no indication that he even understood her question. But in that moment when he looked at her, she knew. Somehow, she knew that the old man had been the one to eliminate the danger that had threatened her.

She let her hand fall to her side. Her smile was polite, sincere. "Thank you.''

Without a word, with the bearing of a king, Victor turned from them and walked away. Toward the woods that were his home.

Lily roused herself and looked at Max. He couldn't be earning all that much money as a sheriff and he had given away several hundred dollars just like that. "Why did you do that?"

Max was trying to remember the last time he saw his bankbook and where he'd put it. "Do what?"

He knew perfectly well what she was talking about. "Offer to pay that man."

"Victor saved April's life when she was a young girl. She was drowning in the lake. If he hadn't jumped in and saved her, she would have died. He never even waited around to be thanked. But that didn't change what he did. Money talks to Jeffords. I knew that if he didn't get restitution, he was going to want to have Victor sent to jail." He watched the man's back as he walked into the woods. "Victor can't be imprisoned."

That sounded almost ominous. "Why, is he some kind of spirit?"

"No, but his spirit would die. A man like Victor can't be contained in four walls. It's not natural for him. He's had enough grief in his life." He saw the way she was looking at him. As if she hadn't seen him before. "What?"

"I'm impressed."

He shrugged. Funny how he hadn't flinched when Jeffords had tried to stare him down, but Lily's gaze had him squirming inside.

"Didn't do it to impress you."

"I know." She was beginning to doubt that the man cared what anyone thought. Which made him very unique in her book. "And that impresses me more." He'd just done something selfless and nice. For the moment, she felt herself softening toward him. "Tell me, Lawman, when was your last good home-cooked meal?" She knew he lived on his own and took his meals at the Salty. "Never mind. I'll cook you one. I owe you." She saw the question in his eyes. "For rescuing me and for not telling everyone what I was wearing at the time or—" There was no point in elaborating. "Anything else."

"None of their business," he told her.

"My sentiments exactly."

"All right," he heard himself agreeing before he entered the jail. It was asking for trouble, but he'd just managed to avert a major catastrophe and felt he owed it to himself to kick back just a little. For now. "I'll pick you up at six."

"But I thought you wanted a home-cooked meal."

"I do. And since you made the suggestion, I get to pick the home." He looked at her. "Mine. Unless you'd rather not."

No, she'd rather. That was just the problem.

You know your problem, Lily? You're a stick-in-the-mud.

She felt her mouth grow a little dry as Allen's words echoed in her head. It grew drier still as she said, "All right."

Chapter Ten

For once, the afternoon was slow at the clinic. Dr. James Quintano, or, as the people in and around Hades referred to him, Dr. Jimmy, took the opportunity to drop in on his sister.

He felt a little guilty that as yet, he hadn't had Lily over to the house for a meal. But that was because it had taken April all this time to get over being intimidated by cooking for a professional chef despite his assurances that Lily wouldn't criticize her.

He drove over to Alison and Luc's house, which was not far out of town, and used the spare key Alison had given him to let himself in. Ordinarily, the door would have remained unlocked. No one locked their doors in Hades, but they did in Seattle and since Lily was there alone, he'd thought to bring his key.

"Hi, Lil," he called out as he walked through the house toward the back.

Jimmy stuck his head in the kitchen. Lily was at the stove, surrounded by boiling pots, more ingredients than he'd thought Alison owned and moving like a whirling dervish.

This was the way he thought of her whenever his thoughts turned to Lily. Perpetual motion surrounded by steam.

"Hi." He grinned, entering. "Thought I'd find you here."

The sound of the door opening had made her jump, but once she heard Jimmy's voice, she'd calmed down. She paused to taste the broth she was making. Salt. Just a pinch, she decided.

Preoccupied, she murmured, "Oh?"

"Yup. Even on vacation." This was the way he remembered home, he thought as he crossed to her. Warm, delicious scents wafting throughout, surrounding him the moment he entered the house. "In your case, Lily, you can't even take the girl out of the kitchen, much less the kitchen out of the girl."

She didn't know if that was a criticism or not; she didn't care. Adding the pinch of salt, she stirred it into the dark liquid, watching it disappear.

"Cooking relaxes me."

It was the only time she felt as if she was completely in control. What she put into something, she got back out of it. Sometimes even more than she'd expected. That didn't work with a relationship. She knew that now. Too many variables, too many unknowns. She'd stick to what she knew and let everyone else venture into romance.

She glanced over toward Jimmy. "Did you come by to harass me?"

"No, I came by, oddly enough, to get you out of the kitchen and into my house." He had to admit that it was like watching an artist work. Mixing, tasting, and mixing again. "April and I thought you might like to come over for dinner."

What did he think she was doing, making mudpies? "I've already got plans."

"Oh?" Sitting on the edge of the counter, he crossed his arms in front of him as if settling in for a long time. At least long enough to get details. "And what plans are those?"

She knew he was prodding her beneath the teasing tone. "Jimmy, I'm the older one here, not you. I don't have to tell you anything."

"True." He inclined his head in agreement. "Grapevine'll take care of that for you." She looked at him sharply. He had her attention, he thought. "You have no idea how quick news travels here. Got the Internet beat by a country mile. 'Course they've had a lot more practice at it, seeing as how civilization comes here at a snail's pace."

She could only shake her head as she measured out the amount of garlic she judged the broth could use. "How do you stand it?"

It had been a long time since he had even thought about that. Now, he considered himself a native. At least by marriage.

"Very well, thanks. It actually suits me, now that I've decided to settle down with a good woman." Jimmy knew exactly what she was doing. He looked at her intently. "But we weren't talking about me."

She arched a brow and gave him a withering look before returning to her work. "We weren't talking about me, either."

"No," he allowed good-naturedly, "but I thought you might take pity on your poor brother, seeing as how if I come home without you, April will grill me within an inch of my life, wanting to know what you're up to. Give me a bone to throw her so she doesn't fillet me."

She wasn't about to tell him that easily. "Tell her I'm cooking."

"I can see that." He paused abruptly, realizing that he'd just been given a clue. "Not for Alison and Luc, I take it."

Rather than answer in the affirmative, Lily merely shrugged a careless response and went about her business.

He pressed his lips together, concentrating. "Well, it has to be for somebody I know because I know everybody here." And then his eyes lit up like sparklers on the Fourth of July. "Max."

Her back to him, Lily almost dropped the ladle into the pot she was stirring. She turned around. Was she that transparent? Or had Max said something after all?

"How did you...I mean—"

He wasn't about to let her launch into a denial.

He'd seen it in her eyes. He'd hit the nail right on the head. Now didn't that just beat all?

"Too late for retractions, Lil." His grin went from ear to ear. He'd always liked the other man. "Max, huh? Damn, this is going to tickle April silly. She never thought Max would give anyone a tumble." He watched his sister, who was stirring madly now, deliberately avoiding looking in his direction. "Hell, for that matter, I was beginning to think I'd have to put aside a room for you in my house—"

That got to her. Jimmy was being insufferable. Is that what he thought? That she was on the midnight express to becoming a spinster? How archaic was that?

"Civilization must have progressed beyond the seventeenth century even up here in Hell on Ice." Her eyes narrowed into dark, angry slits. "There's no need to set aside anything for me, thank you very much." She crossed to the cupboard and took down the flour. "You want to set anything aside, you can have Kevin come live with you. I'm doing just fine on my own." Her anger growing, she set the bag of flour down beside Jimmy's thigh with a thud. A small white cloud rose out of the burlap. "Maybe you've forgotten but until a few weeks ago, I was engaged to be married. That's not exactly spinster material."

"No," he agreed, his eyes meeting hers, "that's window dressing."

He'd lost her. But if he was spoiling for an argument, he'd come to the right place. "Come again?"

He heard the edge in her voice and ignored it. No

matter what words went between them, he loved his sister and wanted only the best for her. Wanted her to have the kind of happiness that had found him, even if it had been quite by accident.

"Let's face it, Lil, Allen was just an excuse, a ruse. You didn't love him." He'd worked with the surgeon, knew the man's reputation as a pompous womanizer. "You couldn't have," he insisted. "You hardly ever spent any time with him. If you had, you would have realized that he wasn't your type or any good for you."

She could feel her temper threatening to erupt and knew that it wasn't entirely Jimmy's fault. Her emotions were just too close to the surface these days. Close to the surface and yet so tightly bundled up she didn't think she would ever be able to unwrap them.

"This is very interesting information to get after the fact, brother dear." She pushed her hair out of her face and began chopping the nuts she'd previously shelled into tiny pieces. "Just where were you when I got engaged to Allen?" Why hadn't he warned her then?

"In church." Eyeing the way she was handling the knife, he moved a little farther down the counter. "Praying you'd come to your senses."

"You never said anything," she accused.

"Could anyone say anything to you?" He asked the question without becoming defensive. It was a given. Lily had always gone her own way. She issued instructions, she didn't follow them. "Could anyone ever tell you anything? Even Kevin."

He hesitated for a second, then decided, because he loved her, that this had to be said. "You were Daddy's little girl, Lily. After Dad died, you blocked out everyone, the three of us included." He saw the protest coming and headed it off. "You didn't do it on purpose, you just did it to keep from getting hurt. We all did that in our own way. Kev threw himself into raising the three of us. I did it by doing stuff that if I caught my own kid doing, I'd tan his hide, and I did it by going out with as many women as I could so that I'd never stop long enough to find the right one."

He smiled, thinking of April. "Lucky thing I came up here to see Alison or I'd probably be working my way across the country by now. And you—" he pinned her with a look "—you handled the hurt by working nonstop at anything you could find. You still do." It wasn't an accusation, just a concern. He hopped off the counter. "Slow down, Lil. Smell the roses. Walk in the moonlight. Let yourself love someone. *Really* love someone."

He could see that he was talking to a stone wall, but he went on anyway. "There are no guarantees in life, Lily, but if you can find that one special person, even five minutes with them is worth the pain that might come later." He knew that he would always be grateful for opening up his heart to April. "And if you get more, so much the better."

He couldn't understand, couldn't possibly understand how devastated she'd been when their father had died so shortly after their mother. She'd felt as if she could never love anyone or anything again, for fear of being abandoned again. She missed her mother, but her father had been her white knight, her world. When he had allowed his broken heart to destroy his spirit despite the fact that she, that they all needed him, she felt as if something within her had died.

Steam was rising from the pot on the rear burner. "Very nice lecture, little brother. But my water's boiling and you're distracting me."

He'd said all he could. The rest would have to take care of itself. "As long as Max distracts you, that's all that counts."

"I didn't actually say it was him," she protested.

"Your pale expression and stuttering said it for you." Jimmy raised his hands and began backing up as she came at him with the ladle. "I'm going, I'm going. Maybe we can make it tomorrow night," he said at the door.

She started to say yes, then remembered her promise to Ike. "Can't."

Jimmy grinned. "Anticipating?" With a hoot of laughter, he ducked as she threw a box of baking soda at his head.

"For your information, I promised Ike I'd make more barbecue sauce for him." There, that should put him in his place, she thought.

"You're settling in nicely."

"I am not settling in," she called after her brother, but he was already gone. With a sigh, she returned to the stove before the broth boiled over.

* * *

Walking in ahead of Max later that evening, Lily looked around the small area he'd told her was the kitchen. There wasn't enough room to turn around twice. Lucky thing she'd prepared everything ahead of time and had brought it with her. She sincerely doubted the man had two pots to bang together.

With a frown, she set the pot she was carrying on the minuscule counter. She'd seen more spacious walk-in closets.

"You call this a kitchen?"

Max placed the large carton filled with tempting smells—almost as tempting as the lady herself, he thought—on the table. It took up the entire surface.

"It's got a stove." He nodded toward it.

The appliance was directly at her back. She spared it a glance.

"So does an appliance warehouse, that doesn't make it a kitchen." Turning around, careful not to knock anything over, she opened the small oven door and looked inside, wondering when it had been last used. It smelled more than a little stale. "It's what you do with the stove that counts."

"Okay." He gestured toward the appliance gamely. "Do something with it."

She fully intended to, to warm up the crepes she'd created, but she continued to look at the interior dubiously. "Will some furry creature come scurrying out if I turn it on?"

He laughed, taking no offense. He took most of his meals at the Salty, or went over to either April's or his grandmother's. He knew better than to eat at June's. "Only one way to find out."

Washing her hands in the sink, she looked around for a towel. There was one hanging haphazardly on the side of the sink. "I notice you're not trying to pretend that you've used this recently."

He liked watching her take charge, he thought. "I don't believe in lying."

She nodded, taking care to hang the towel back up. "Admirable."

He didn't know about admirable. To him it was a matter of practical more than anything else. "Too confusing trying to keep your stories straight. Lesson I learned as a kid."

That gave her a instant image. "The town's bad boy grows up to be the sheriff?"

She'd picked up on that. A glint of admiration entered his eyes. "Something like that. It puts me one step ahead of kids who act the way I did." Max stepped closer to her and looked around. No two ways about it, the kitchen was a snug fit, but he wasn't complaining. "Okay, what do you want me to do?"

If she took a deep breath, she would bump into him. "Stay out of my way."

He looked around. The whole place was small, but then, he didn't require all that much. A bed, a place to hang his hat and somewhere to make his coffee in the morning. Anything else was just luxury. "That might not be too easy."

Most of the work had been done, but she still

needed room to heat things up. "Why don't you set the table?"

He looked toward the small table that sat four as long as nobody minded their knees getting friendly. "Can't. You've got the carton on it."

She sighed, frustrated. "Then I guess you can just hang around while I get things ready."

She was doing all the work. Wanting to play the host, at least moderately, he turned around and opened the refrigerator. He nearly bumped into her as he bent over. "Like a beer?"

She hadn't had beer in a long time, not since she'd been in college. But right now, it sounded good to her. Sorting through the carton Max had carried in, she put her hand out in his general direction. It wasn't much of a stretch.

"I'll take that as a yes." Taking out two bottles, Max popped first one top, then the other. He handed the first to her. But rather than take a drag from his own bottle, he took a deep whiff of what she had begun stirring on the stove. "Smells good. What are you making, or is that a secret?"

"No secret." She was glad she'd thought to bring a large baking pan to heat everything up in. It didn't look as if Max owned one. "Tonight's main course will be Crepe à la Lily."

He took a pull from the bottle, his eyes on her lips. He wouldn't mind nibbling on something that had her name on it. Wouldn't mind nibbling on her, either. "Sounds complicated."

She intended it to. But since he was family, in a

manner of speaking, she let him in on the secret. "The trick to good cooking is to take something simple and dress it up—and make everyone think you've just performed a miracle in the kitchen."

Setting down the bottle, he found himself moving closer to her as she worked, drawn as if by some force he couldn't resist even though he knew he should. "You know, you really didn't have to do this."

She shrugged, trying to remain nonchalant. Trying not to think about how close he was. And how she wanted him closer still.

"I know. I just wanted to say thank you. After all, you did rescue me from the bear."

Standing behind her, he caught himself as he reached out to stroke her hair and pulled his hand back. "Victor did that."

The man was more upstanding than Dudley Do-right, she thought in exasperation.

"All right, rescued me from the tree, then." She turned, only to find that there was nowhere to go. Words came faster, mimicking the rate of her pulse. "I think I was too petrified to come down again. If you hadn't climbed up to get me down, I might still be stuck in it."

The smile curled along his lips like seduction as he moved his head from side to side slowly.

"Not in this town you wouldn't. As soon as word got out that a beautiful woman was stuck in the tree, you would have had so many miners and lumberjacks milling around you they would have formed their own human ladder and net to catch you."

She didn't care about miners and lumberjacks. The only thing on her mind was a very sexy lawman. "Can't you let me just say thank you?"

He took the ladle from her lax fingers and placed it on the counter. "There're simpler ways to do that."

"Like?" she whispered, unable to tear her eyes away from his.

"This," he answered, the word gliding along her nerves, seducing her. And then he bent his head and touched his lips to hers.

Lily's head instantly began to spin.

Madly.

Before it spun away from her completely, she reached out to the side and felt around for the knobs on the stove. The ones she'd just turned on. With a twist, she turned both off. She didn't want the house to burn down and she had a feeling that she wasn't coming back to the stove anytime soon.

At least she fervently hoped not.

He'd only wanted to kiss her. Had wanted to kiss her ever since he'd been alone with her in the woods. Max had had time to think all of this through, had had time to give himself all the reasons why this shouldn't be happening between them. It was a long list.

Except that he had to kiss her. Had to hold her. Had to make love with her or find himself turning into one of those hermits who talked to squirrels and trees and shied away from people.

When Lily leaned her body into his, she felt as if an all-important chunk had been taken out of the dam.

Suddenly, desire flooded through her. Desire that threatened to sweep her away.

What was more, she didn't care. She *wanted* to be swept away. *Wanted* to glory in this overwhelming sensation that had found her.

She'd never felt this need with Allen.

With anyone.

Cupping the back of her head, Max tilted it so that his mouth could feast on hers. So that he could kiss the sweet column of her neck and lose himself in the scent of her hair.

An edginess spilled through his veins. What he felt was slipping dangerously beyond his control.

That should have worried him, but it didn't. All he could think of was this woman in his arms. This longing in his body. He needed one to answer the other.

His hands splayed around her waist, holding her to him. He kissed her over and over again as if she were the very sustenance he'd been waiting for for so long.

He tasted her sigh on his lips and it fired him. He wanted to make love with her.

But still, he felt that he couldn't allow this to go further if she had any doubts. With effort that bordered on the superhuman, he pulled his head away and looked at her. ''Are you sure, Lily?''

No, she wasn't sure. Wasn't sure of anything. But she did know that she was tired of sitting on the fence, tired of wanting to feel something and not feeling anything. She was feeling something now and she wanted to act on it before it disappeared.

Exasperated, she raised herself up on her toes, her

body pressed against his. "Stop being the sheriff for once in your life and just kiss me."

A man couldn't do more than that, he thought. Even if he was the law for more than two hundred miles. The taste of her mouth was too sweet, the soft impression of her body too compelling. He'd given Lily her chance and she'd refused it. Thank God.

His arms closing around her, Max kissed her as if their very souls depended on it. As if she were the first woman he had really felt anything for.

Because she was.

Because of what he had seen as a child, because of the father who had walked out on them, leaving his mother broken and grieving in his wake, Max'd had no use for relationships. He'd never allowed himself to feel anything beyond pleasure before.

There were feelings here, feelings he hadn't encountered before, feelings he didn't understand. And what was worse, he had no control here. He had no say, no way of *not* allowing himself to feel for Lily. Control, permission, free will had all been usurped by a force that could not be tamed, could not be defeated.

His soul was on fire and she had the matches. It was as simple as that.

Lifting her in his arms, his mouth still sealed to hers, Max carried her to the small room that served as his bedroom. Gently, he placed her on the bed that seemed to take up the entire room.

Max watched her eyes as he lay down next to her and knew that he was completely lost. She owned the moment and him.

Chapter Eleven

Just as Max brought his mouth down to hers, the annoying ringing started. It was coming from her pocket, from her cell phone.

Max pulled his head back. His lips curved in amusement. Maybe this was some kind of sign.

"I think that's for you."

Frustration drummed through her as Lily sat up and pulled out the phone. She flipped it open and without waiting to hear a single word from the person on the other end—though there was no doubt in her mind that it was Arthur—said, "Not now," before hitting the disconnect button and tossing the phone across the room.

Granted it wasn't a great distance away, but it was beyond her reach, which was all that counted. She wouldn't feel obligated to pick up the next call, which probably would follow on the heels of this aborted one.

With a sigh, she looked up at Max and murmured, "Where were we?"

Max grinned. "I'm impressed," he said, gathering her to him once again.

Just having him so close to her made minivolcanoes erupt inside of her. Her eyes held his as they both lay down once more. "And I'm a woman about to go up in smoke at any moment."

"Then we don't have any more moments to waste," he told her just before he brought his mouth back down to hers.

Desire, renewed, hit an instant before his lips touched hers, taking possession of him.

Sealing his fate.

It was all Max could do to school himself to go slowly, gently, and not completely lose himself in this sensation slamming against his body with the force of a tsunami.

It was a storm all right, he thought. A storm of emotion, of needs, the likes of which he had never encountered before.

Max had no time to analyze what it was that Lily did to him, he could only hold on and hope to survive at journey's end.

And if he didn't, well, it wouldn't be the worst way to go.

As his mouth made love to hers, his hands found their way beneath her tank top. His fingers curved along her skin, exploring, caressing, memorizing the soft, pliant flesh.

He could feel her breasts ripening beneath his touch even through the thin, lacy bra she wore. One snap of his thumb and forefinger and the bra began to slip from her body.

Lily shivered. With warmth, with anticipation. With desire.

Her heart racing, she clung to him, pressing her body closer as it heated.

So this was what it was like, making love with a man. Being wanted by a man.

Wanting a man. Because her body yearned for his.

This was what she'd had in mind when she'd gone to Allen's apartment that day. She'd planned for the impromptu picnic to end this way, with her giving herself to him, surrendering to sensations, to an experience that had been waiting for her behind the mists all these years. She'd been a virgin then, she was a virgin now. A virgin in search of fulfillment.

And now she'd found it, found it here in the middle of a forgotten, all but godforsaken wilderness. Would miracles never cease?

If Lily thought she would lose courage at the last minute, she was happily surprised. Rather than lose courage, she felt herself infused with it.

Desire throbbed in her veins so strong that it took away all her thoughts, all her inhibitions. All she wanted was to be his in every sense of the word. And the sooner the better.

But as she rushed toward her destiny, he slowed his pace.

Max cupped her cheek, a sweetness traveling through him he couldn't begin to identify.

"Shh, we have all evening, Lily. Slowly, slowly," he cautioned as her hands raced along his body, tugging at his shirt, fumbling at the buckle on his belt.

But even as he told her to slow down, he found it wasn't easy reining himself in. Not when all he wanted to do was to drive himself into her, to bury himself in her sweetness and to feel that all-powerful, empowering surge pulsing through his veins.

Moving away just a fraction of an inch, he tugged at the hem of the tank top that still covered her, then brought it up over her head and tossed it aside. The bra sighed away on its own.

Something stirred within him just to look at her.

Max covered her breasts with his hands, and then with his lips. Lily squirmed beneath him in response, arching her body to his. Enflaming him further.

His heart racing, he rose to his knees. Taking her hands in his, he brought her up with him. Quickly shedding his shirt, he fixed his fingers on the rim of her jeans, slowly running his thumb along the inside, skimming the skin just below her navel. He could feel her anticipation.

Each breath she took drove him a little higher, made him want her a little more.

The rest became a blur, though he tried to remember each moment clearly later. Clothes found their way to the floor, beside the banished cell phone. And then their naked bodies tangled together as they fell back on the bed, reveling in the inflammable first moments of new discovery.

If an ounce of timidity or shyness still existed within her, Lily forced herself beyond it as her hands slid along his hard, sleek body.

She couldn't touch him enough, couldn't want him enough.

Her body was slick with anticipation as he kissed her over and over again, bringing his lips along the slopes and curves of her soft flesh as it quivered with each contact.

A complete novice in the mysteries of lovemaking, Lily mimicked him, touching as he touched, kissing as he kissed. Following his lead until her own instincts, instincts she hadn't known she possessed until this very moment, gave her the courage to initiate movements of her own, to take the lead from him whenever possible.

It became a competition to see who could give whom the most pleasure. And all the while, their hold on restraint continued to lessen. Lessen to such a degree that the final moment came closer and closer, rushing toward them on winged feet.

And then, knowing that if he held back one more second he would completely explode, Max pushed her back on the bed and parted her legs with his knee. Her breath catching in her throat, Lily opened for him, wrapping her legs around his.

He began to drive himself into her and then stopped

as unexpected resistance met his entry. His eyes widened as he looked at her.

For a moment, he didn't understand.

And then he did.

"Lily?"

He was going to stop. Her heart quickened in disappointment. In dread. He couldn't stop. She couldn't let him, Lily thought frantically. If he stopped now, she was going to die, right here, right now. The rejection would be too much for her to bear.

Raising her head, Lily caught his lips against her own, pressing hard, coaxing him further as she raised her hips higher against him.

He heard her mute entreaty, felt himself lose his own battle with what he knew in his heart was right. Swept away by her assault on his senses, he drove himself into her.

There was only hesitation at the first moment, when her eyes flew open. Her body shuddered at the impact. But then, to keep him from retreating, her hands closed around his back, clinging.

In a heartbeat, she matched the rhythm he'd begun. Faster and faster they went until he crested. She followed less than half a second later. A wild cry of surprise and exhilaration escaped her lips.

Slowly, as the warmth of the moment began to recede, the cold reality of what he had just done penetrated, skewering his conscience.

Feeling like a heel, Max rolled off her. He was unsure whether he should gather her to him and hold her the way he wanted to, or refrain and try to pull the pieces together.

It shouldn't have happened this way.

Unable to face her, he looked up at the heavily beamed ceiling above his bed. "Why didn't you tell me?"

She felt the knife drive itself into her heart. She bit her lower lip to keep the tears that suddenly sprang up into her eyes at bay.

Staring up at the same ceiling, Lily asked woodenly, "Tell you what?"

Communing with the ceiling wasn't going to get him anywhere. He'd done it, now it was time to face up to his responsibility.

Max raised himself up on one elbow to look at her. Accusations were not going to right the wrong that had been done. He needed to apologize.

He wanted to hold her, to make it better. He didn't know how. "It wasn't supposed to happen like that."

He couldn't have said anything worse. She bit down harder on her lip. "Are you apologizing to me or yourself?"

The question took him aback. He blinked, not sure what she was talking about. "To you. Why would I be apologizing to myself?"

That much she though was obvious. "Because you let yourself make love to an untried virgin. Expecting a symphony, you got someone playing a comb wrapped in tissue paper."

"What the hell are you babbling about?" he demanded angrily.

The anger was directed at himself, but she had no way of knowing that. Hurt, she turned away from him and got up. Trying to see her clothes through tears that she refused to shed. Tears that were blinding her vision anyway.

"Don't bother 'apologizing,'" she retorted. "I don't want your damn apology."

He hadn't a clue what she was carrying on about, he only worried that he'd hurt her. "I don't know what the hell you're talking about—symphonies and tissue paper." None of it made any sense to him. "I just know that a woman's first time is supposed to be with someone who counts."

"And you don't."

She assumed that was what he meant. That he didn't count and that he didn't want to count. She saw Max begin to answer, knowing in her heart that the answer would have something to do with their being literally worlds apart and she'd be returning to hers shortly. She didn't want to hear it. Any of it.

"Don't you think it's up to the woman to decide who she wants her first time to be with?" she demanded.

"Yes." Sitting up, he dragged his hand through his hair. How could she be a virgin? "I don't understand. You were engaged—"

"I was busy," she snapped, then realized how terribly lame that excuse had to sound.

How terribly lame it actually *was*.

Maybe she'd always been so busy because she was afraid to consummate anything, afraid to commit her body and heart where her mind had told her to go. She didn't know, but all that was behind her now and didn't count anymore. What had just happened, did. For better or for worse.

"Fortunately," she added, the tiniest of smiles finding its way to her lips. "Otherwise, my first time would have been with a first-class rat." Her eyes softened as she looked at him. "Instead of you."

"Lily." Fighting mixed feelings that were even now beginning to give way to desire, Max reached for her hand and pulled her back to bed. "You should have told me."

Not really wanting to rush out, she let herself be pulled back.

"And just where in the conversation could I have worked that in? 'Hand me the cayenne pepper—oh, and yes, by the way, I'm a virgin.'" She laughed shortly at the absurdity of it all. "For God's sake, you people don't even *have* enough cayenne pepper up here, how could I hope that you'd understand why I am the way I am?"

He didn't see how one had anything to do with the other, but it didn't matter. "I didn't have to understand, I just had to know."

"So that, what? You could toss me aside, knowing that you wouldn't get your money's worth if you continued to make love to me?"

"Where the hell did you get that ridiculous notion from? And what makes you think that you were the slightest bit lacking? You weren't. You should have told me you were a virgin so that at the very least, I could make it memorable for you."

Lily caught her lower lip between her teeth, looking at him. Tears came out of nowhere, filling her. Tears not of disappointment, but of a strange, heady joy. "And what makes you think you didn't?"

The words, low, whispered, seductively moved along his skin. Making him want her all over again. Damn, but she did have some kind of power over him. "You make it awfully hard for a man to just walk away."

"Then don't," she entreated softly, her hand on his arm, her eyes on his. "Don't walk away."

It was all the encouragement he needed.

"Suddenly," he told her as he took her into his arms, "I can't move."

It was then that she grinned at him, the moment flowering into a bouquet of possibilities, the hurt vanishing as if it had all been just a bad dream, best forgotten.

"You'd better," she warned with a laugh before she sealed her lips to his.

He watched her get dressed.

His temperature cooling, his logic returning, Max still couldn't drag his eyes away from the pleasurable sight. Lily Quintano was a beautiful woman, with or without clothing.

Pulling on his trousers, Max stooped to pick up her cell phone. As his hand closed over it, it all but danced in his palm.

He looked at her quizzically as he offered the small item to her. "I'm not sure, but I think your phone's shivering."

Still encased in a euphoric haze, Lily was in no hurry to answer it. "I put it on vibrate before I tossed it aside."

He glanced around to see where his shirt had landed. "Maybe you'd better answer it and put Arthur out of his misery."

It continued to vibrate. "How do you know it's Arthur?"

He grinned, picking up his shirt. "I'm the sheriff. I know these things."

As she flipped the phone open, Max dropped his shirt back to the floor. Coming up behind her, he encircled her waist with his arms and pulled her to him.

About to speak, Lily could feel Max's hard, smooth chest against her back. It took effort to concentrate. It took more effort not to sigh.

"Hello?"

"Where have you been?" Arthur demanded in a plaintive whine. "I've been monitoring all the news channels, listening for avalanche or earthquake reports." He huffed, his voice cracking. "I thought you were dead."

A sliver of guilt found its way into the afterglow that was blanketing her. "Trouble with reception," she lied.

Arthur clearly was in the dark. "What did you mean by 'not now' then?" he whined. "I heard you say that just before the connection suddenly went down.''

"Can't remember," she answered blithely. "Why don't you tell me why you called before we lose the connection again?"

Behind her, she could feel Max lifting her hair from her neck. Before she could turn her head to ask him what he was doing, she felt his lips against her nape. Kissing her. Scrambling her thoughts.

Her heart began to drum so loudly, she had trouble hearing Arthur.

"I need to know if I should go ahead and order two hundred and fifty squab for the Douglas reception next month? Or do you want to do it when you get back?" he added hopefully.

Get back.

Lily didn't want to think about that. She still had a week's vacation left and she wanted to concentrate on that. Getting back did not hold the allure it had held just a few hours ago.

"You do it, Arthur." She heard the nervous intake of breath on the other end of the line. "You'll do fine. Just make sure you keep a diary."

"A diary?" Max asked as she terminated the call a few minutes later. He took the phone from her and tossed it onto his discarded shirt. "Just how old did you say this Arthur was?"

"I meant as in everything he does at the restaurant. I don't want to go back to a disaster."

He nodded, not wanting to think about anything beyond the moment.

It seemed so odd to him, feeling that way. He'd always believed in living each moment as it came, but he knew that the present moment rested in the foundation of the moments that had come before and was a stepping stone to the moments, hours, days, that were to come after.

Now he wanted nothing but the moment. Divested of anything else. Because anything else meant that she would be gone.

He nibbled on her ear, then looked at her just as she shivered, a sexy look in his eyes. "So, as I recall, you promised me dinner."

It took a moment to work her heart out of her throat. "You're hungry?" she asked in disbelief.

"Starved," he said. The next moment, to prove it, he kissed her.

Excitement pulsed in her veins as she pulled her head back to look at him. "And just what is it you have in mind for the main course?"

His hands slid all along her body as he molded her to him. "Guess."

She didn't have to guess. She knew. He wanted the same thing she did. Maybe she *hadn't* been the inadequate lover she'd been so afraid she would be.

Mischief danced in her eyes as she pretended to protest. "But we just got dressed."

He was already undoing the clasp at her bra, his hands moving so as to catch the soft flesh that was newly freed from its confinement. He saw desire flicker in her eyes, felt his own rise further.

"The really great thing about clothes is that they

work both ways. You don't have to stick with them once you have them on. They can come right off again.'' He reached for the hem of her tank top. ''Let me give you a demonstration.''

He didn't get to finish what he was saying. Lily brushed her lips against his and suddenly all words became unnecessary.

There was only now, and each other. Nothing else mattered or existed beyond that.

It was enough.

Chapter Twelve

It wasn't enough. Not nearly enough. What in heaven's name had she been thinking?

Trying to get a grip on the sudden spike in her temper, Lily threw another section of spareribs on the cutting board and picked up the cleaver.

Yes, it had been wonderful, no question about it. As a first, last, in-between experience, making love with Max had been fantastic, but now it was in her past and it resided there as a mistake.

She brought down the cleaver with a vengeance, separating one section of meat from another in a clean, sharp cut.

What you don't know, you can't miss, only in theory, but not in actuality. And now she knew. Knew what it was like to make exquisite love with a man.

She brought the cleaver down again. *Whack!*

A rotten man.

As Lily swung the meat cleaver down hard on the cutting board again, the kitchen in the saloon resounded with the noise.

She'd finally gotten into Max's kitchen last night to warm up the all-but-forgotten meal when there'd been a knock on his door. Hurrying to get things ready, she'd been startled to hear a woman's voice. A very young woman's voice.

Her heart had constricted even before she'd walked out into the living area to see Vanessa standing in the doorway. Max had just grabbed her parka and was pushing it back onto her body. Her very supple, very nude body.

The anger that had flashed over her in that instant had all but blinded Lily. It was the incident in Allen's apartment all over again.

How could she have been so stupid as to think that anything could be different out here?

Especially out here, she underscored mentally, picking up yet another rack of spareribs. Out here men hungered for women like they thirsted for beer.

More, because there was more beer to be had than women.

Trying to keep her mind on what she was doing, Lily pressed her lips together to hold back the unexpected sob that rose up in her throat. Had to be the onions she'd been chopping. Couldn't be because of the man. He damn well wasn't worth it.

Everything had happened quickly after that.

She remembered gasping. Max had swung around to look at her then, surprise and guilt in his eyes. There'd been a smug look on the young girl's face.

That was when she'd seen the keys on the side table. Grabbing them, she'd run out and commandeered his vehicle, not caring if it was official property or not. He and that minutes-from-being-underage plaything of his could stay there and freeze to death in each other's arms for all she cared.

Too bad it was summer, she remembered thinking. If there'd been any justice in heaven, it would have been the height of winter.

She'd heard Max calling her name, but she hadn't even bothered to turn around. She'd just wanted to get away.

Muttering to herself, she paused to stir first one giant pot on the stove, then another before returning to the cutting board.

Whack!

This morning, she'd given Alison no explanation as to why she'd returned without her pots, said nothing about why Max's vehicle had been parked in front of their house. She'd planned to just keep to herself the entire day. She would have gone silently into the night, as well, but Ike had come by to take her up on her promise. Overriding her feeble protest, he'd brought her to the Salty.

The best thing for her, actually. The only therapy that worked.

With another mighty swing that was far too energetic for the small piece of meat on the cutting board,

Lily brought the cleaver down on the spareribs. One side nearly popped off the board, but she grabbed it just in time. Taking both severed pieces, she threw them into the pot.

They hit the metal side first with a jarring noise before sinking into the bubbling sauce.

There seemed to be no dissipating the anger within her. Lily picked another rack out of the opened bag next to her on the counter and threw it on the board.

"Have those spareribs done something to offend you, darlin'?"

Startled, the cleaver halted in midswing, she looked up to see Ike standing in the doorway of the kitchen. His arms crossed in front of him, he was observing her. There was a mildly amused look on his face. She had absolutely no idea how long he'd been standing there watching her and decided she cared even less.

"What are you talking about?" she asked tersely. She swung the cleaver down again. The noise the blow made echoed in her chest.

Exercising a measure of caution, Ike moved into the room slowly. His kitchen help had long since fled the area, saying something about not wanting to be in the same room with "that crazy woman." That was when Ike had decided to do a little investigating on his own.

He nodded toward the pot. "I just thought, the way you're slamming them around on the cutting board, they might have done something to offend you and you're putting them in their place."

She wasn't in the mood for his charm. "I'm just cutting the meat," she said between clenched teeth.

"If those spareribs were human, I'd say you were declaring war on them. Or someone." He was standing in front of her now, trying to read her expression. Something was definitely troubling her. "Care to talk about it?"

She didn't even look up. Her eyes were on the cleaver as she worked. "No."

He was tempted to catch her hand midswing, but since he was partial to both his arms remaining just where they were, he refrained. "Then there is something to talk about."

Lily set her jaw hard as cleaver and board connected. "No."

The hell there wasn't. He hadn't spent the last decade behind the bar, listening to men and the occasional member of the fairer sex, spill out their insides without becoming incredibly familiar with the signs.

"You know how a volcanic eruption comes about, darlin'?"

This time she did raise her eyes to him. "Don't worry, you won't get drenched in lava."

Ike's eyes met hers for a moment before she brought her head down again. "Wasn't myself I was worrying about, darlin'."

Blowing out a breath, she paused to push her hair off of her face, and looked at him accusingly. "Why would you worry about me?"

Ike felt he had a better question for her. "Why shouldn't I?"

She hated when people turned questions around like that. "I'm not family."

He laughed softly at her answer and she felt like a kindergartner who'd gotten her numbers confused.

"Darlin', out here, we're all family—like it or not. Come winter, until they get that transporter stuff from 'Star Trek' perfected, we're all we have."

About to ignore him and get back to what she was doing, his answer caught her by surprise. "You know about 'Star Trek'?"

Ike smiled. Hades was struggling, but it was definitely coming along and had more than a good toehold in the twenty-first century. But a great many people still thought it was something out of the eighteen hundreds.

"This isn't the end of the world, darlin'." He leaned a hip against the table where she'd been cutting the meat. "Though I admit that sometimes it feels that way." He winked at her. "Could also feel like the beginning of the world. It's all in the way you look at things."

Straightening, he crossed to the stove and paused to dip just the tiniest tip of his forefinger into the sauce. He stuck it into his mouth.

"Mmm, good." He nodded, well pleased, then brushed his hand off on the back of his jeans. "Well, I'll leave you to your work. Make sure you take a few prisoners," he nodded at the all-but-depleted bag of meat. "The boys out front are getting restless."

With a short nod of her head, Lily got back to her work, saying nothing.

As she cut up the last rack of spareribs, she decided that as soon as she got the opportunity, she was going to call the airlines and change her ticket. There was no reason to remain out here for another week. If she wanted to be humiliated, she could always do it closer to home and with far less inconvenience.

Max debated letting the whole thing blow over. But Lily would be gone within a week and he didn't want to end things on such a sour note.

Still, he wasn't used to explaining himself. He was what he was and expected people to take him that way, expected them to know that when a bad light was cast on him, that was all it was, a bad light. That he had nothing to do with the shadowing.

Just as he'd had nothing to do with Vanessa showing up on his doorstep last night.

He'd come to the door when he'd heard someone knocking, preoccupied, wrestling with the completely unfamiliar feelings that were battering his soul, and pulled it open. He'd had absolutely no idea who could be at his door at that time of night and Vanessa was the last person he'd expected to find there.

She'd smiled up at him with that smile she'd been practicing, the one that peeled the socks off the younger men. The one that, had he not had the standards he did, might have peeled his socks off, as well.

"Hi," she'd purred. "I thought you might want some company."

It never ceased to amaze Max how some people couldn't pick up on signals when he'd been working off signals for most of his life. Vanessa, for instance, was oblivious to the ones he'd tried subtly to give her.

"Vanessa," he'd begun, hoping to send her on her way before Lily came into the room, "I'm a little busy right now. Go on home."

He remembered the glint that entered the girl's eyes. That should have warned him, and had he been thinking clearly, it very well might have. But his mind had been on the woman in the kitchen.

"Sure you want me to do that?" Vanessa had purred.

The next thing he knew, she'd dropped the parka from her shoulders. As it began to slide down her arms, he'd realized that she hadn't a stitch of clothing on underneath.

He'd grabbed the parka before it could get past her hips and slid it back up her arms with a jerk.

"I'm sure," he'd informed her sternly.

That was when he'd heard Lily gasp. The next thing he knew, she'd run by him. Run by him uttering only one word in her wake.

"Bastard."

She hadn't stopped to listen to a single word from him.

Hurrying after her, he saw her climb into his Jeep and drive off. Part of him had wanted to jump into Vanessa's vehicle and chase Lily down. But the other part of him had balked at having to explain himself, at being convicted without so much as an indictment, much less a trial.

What did he want with a woman who couldn't even give him the benefit of the doubt?

Everything, it seemed. Because he'd been wrestling with his emotions all night, followed by more of the same today.

He'd hustled a pouting Vanessa into her car, threatening to tie her hands behind her back if she so much as tried to take her parka off again or to reach for him. Thwarted, the girl had sat in the back seat, fuming, calling him names.

"Just what the hell does she have that I don't?" Vanessa had demanded.

He wasn't about to get into that with her. He knew how badly damaged the girl's self-esteem really was beneath that bravado.

"Right now, my car. I want you to get it into your head, Vanessa, I'm too old for you. You can't force a person to have feelings for you when they're not there. I think of you as my little sister."

She'd cursed roundly in response.

His eyes had met hers in the rearview mirror. "Someone should have cared enough to wash your mouth out with soap a long time ago, Vanessa."

She turned in her seat, the top of her parka parting slightly. "Don't you find me pretty?"

"You're more than pretty, Vanessa, but it takes more than that for anything to happen between two people." He'd heard her sigh. "Don't sell yourself short," he'd told her. And then he paused before continuing. "I don't usually say this, but maybe you should start thinking about leaving Hades, going somewhere else and starting a new life.''

''Maybe I will,'' she'd snapped angrily.

Vanessa hadn't said another word until he'd brought her home. When he'd gotten out of the car, she was still sitting in it, pouting. Maybe hoping he'd change his mind about the offer she'd initially made in his cabin.

He'd left the keys in the ignition.

From there, Max had walked the two and a half miles to Alison and Luc's house. He'd been relieved to see that his Jeep was parked out front. That meant that Lily had gotten home safely.

The relief quickly turned to anger as he thought of the way Lily had run out of the cabin without giving him so much as a single chance to say anything in his own defense. In the blink of an eye, she'd conducted her own kangaroo court and found him guilty.

He'd stewed about it all night and most of today, his disposition turning more and more surly. He'd walked into the Salty less than three minutes ago and ordered a stiff drink, not that he thought it would do him any good, but he was officially off the clock— as off the clock as a sheriff could be when he was the only law in the area—and he felt he owed it to himself to unwind.

''She's inside if you want to talk to her,'' Ike said to him without missing a step as he walked around to the side of the bar.

Max took a long hit of his drink before he turned

around to look at Ike. "What makes you think I want to talk to anyone?"

One side of Ike's generous mouth rose higher than the other.

"Hey, standing behind this bar, you get to be half father confessor, half psychic. But in this case, just being brighter than a potato would have led me to the conclusion I just reached."

Ike leaned over the bar, placing one hand on Max's shoulder. "But one word of warning, friend." He glanced back toward the kitchen. The noise had stopped. Temporarily. "Woman's got a meat cleaver in her hand and from the way she's swinging it, she *really* knows how to use it. I'd stand in the doorway doing my talking if I were you."

Max spent exactly five seconds debating his next course of action. Throwing back the rest of his drink, he placed his glass on the bar and then approached the kitchen in purposeful strides.

Watching, Ike could only shake his head. He'd been betting it would only take Max three.

Opening the door, Max saw that Lily was alone in the small, steamy kitchen. It felt at least fifteen degrees hotter in here than it was in the bar.

It figured, seeing as how he felt he had one foot in hell.

Stepping inside, he let the swinging door close behind him before saying anything. "Why did you run out last night?"

She knew he'd come.

She'd been bracing herself all evening, all day.

With a pronounced swing that had the cleaver almost cutting into the board, as well, she didn't even bother to look up. "I don't do threesomes."

He felt like grabbing her shoulders and shaking her. The surge of anger surprised him. He hadn't felt this angry since he'd watched his mother pine away for his father, not listening to any of her children's pleas to "be like you used to, Mama." The helpless feeling had made him impotently furious.

"Neither do I." His words were measured out tersely.

Lily jerked up her head, her eyes accusing. "So what was she, the second shift? Or did the promise of fresh meat just make you forget to tell her you were going to be entertaining?"

It wasn't easy curbing his temper or the words that sprang to his lips. But matching her retort for retort wasn't going to solve anything, or clear this up. And he wanted it cleared.

"I didn't forget to tell her because I don't tell her anything. She wasn't the second shift, she wasn't the first shift and, before you ask, she wasn't *any* shift."

Lily threw the cleaver down. The blade hit the side of the board and fell off the table to the floor. Lily narrowly sidestepped it, but didn't miss a beat of her anger.

"Oh, then she just appeared on your doorstep like that?"

What did it take to get that through her thick head? "Yes."

Lily fisted her hands at her hips. Did he think she

was an idiot? "Barefoot up to the neck for no reason at all."

"Oh, she has a reason all right," he contradicted, barely keeping his own voice under control. If this turned into a shouting match, the kitchen would be filled to overflowing with nosy miners and lumberjacks in no time. "She's trying to rub it in her father's face."

"Making love with you," Lily sneered.

"Making love to anyone," he emphasized. "It doesn't matter who." His eyes narrowed. He'd had enough. He didn't even know what he was doing here. "And not that it's any business of yours, but I haven't even held her hand. I've just tried to keep her out of trouble, but that doesn't seem to be working."

For just a moment, there was something in his eyes that almost made her believe him. "Not much of a negotiator, are you?"

The sigh was angry, frustrated. "Doesn't look that way." He took a step back. "I just wanted you to know."

With that, Max turned to walk out.

She bit her lip, telling herself that she didn't believe him, telling herself to just let him walk away.

But the man had such a straight back...

Straight as an arrow, was what Jimmy had said about him.

"I surprised Allen that way."

He stopped, just as his hand was on the swinging door, ready to push it open. Against his better judgment, he turned around again.

"What, wearing a parka?"

She shook her head. She shouldn't even be telling him this. Why let someone else in on her humiliation? But if he was on the level and she'd maligned him...

"No, coming to his apartment with a picnic lunch. Finding him in bed with another woman..." Hesitating, she ran her tongue along her dried lips. "Seeing Vanessa standing there like that last night just brought everything back to me." She lowered her eyes, not wanting to see pity in his at the impromptu confession. "Made me feel like a fool."

Before he could think better of it, Max crossed to her. "Just because your fiancé is an idiot doesn't make you a fool."

"Ex-fiancé," she corrected with feeling. Even saying that rankled. How could she had been so stupid, so blind? And why hadn't Jimmy said anything to him about Allen's reputation? Was she really such a dragon lady?

She knew the answer to that and it bothered her.

Max gave a short, sharp nod of his head. "So much the better." The brief moment of vulnerability he'd glimpsed in her eyes had him softening instantly. "But in either case, what someone else does doesn't make you a fool. Just because that guy didn't know a good thing when he had it, that's no reflection on you."

She wanted to ask him how he could say that, how he could profess that she was a "good thing" when she'd all but separated him from his head? Instead she asked, "And what about Vanessa?"

Suspicion raised its head. Were they going to go around about the girl again? "What about her?"

"Well, from what I saw," Lily began with a smattering of caution, beginning to believe in his innocence, "Vanessa seemed to think you'd welcome her coming over like that."

"No," he contradicted, "she *hoped* I would." He was surprised she didn't know about Vanessa yet. Stories made the rounds quickly. He would have thought she would have heard by now. "Vanessa is a sad little girl whose mother died when she was very young and whose father never paid any attention to her, other than to have her wait on him hand and foot. Vanessa was a very plain little girl, but when she turned fifteen, she blossomed."

Lily couldn't help wondering just how much of that "blossoming" Max had noticed and how he had viewed it.

"Suddenly a lot of people were paying attention to her and she got her head turned around."

"By a lot of people," Lily echoed. "Are you in that crowd?"

For the first time since he'd opened the door to Vanessa last night, Max allowed himself a smile.

"I make it a habit of never being in a crowd. That way, you don't get hurt if there's a sudden stampede." He took off his hat and held it as he looked at what was going on in the closest pot. "Now, how long are you going to be working on those things?"

She didn't even have to look. "The first batch is almost ready. Why, are you hungry?"

He pretended that his hunger was restricted to food and not the woman who had been on his mind these past twenty-four hours.

"Well, as I remember, you still didn't give me that meal you promised. By the way, I brought the pots back to Alison just before I came here." He'd done it hoping to find her. That was when Alison had told him where Lily had gone.

She nodded. "All right," she decided out loud, "you get the first taste."

He smiled at her as he looked into her eyes. "I've already found out I like being the first."

Lily turned to reach for a ladle. But before she could begin to give him a serving, Max swept her into his arms and kissed her.

Making the kitchen and the immediate world fade away.

Chapter Thirteen

"Hey, no squeezing the cook," Ike warned, walking in.

Like a spring that had suddenly been released, Lily jumped back, away from Max. Flustered at being caught in a totally unguarded moment, it took her a moment to compose herself.

Smoothing down her apron, she turned and reached for a ladle.

"That's 'chef,'" she corrected tersely.

Why had Ike picked this minute to walk in? She'd just begun sinking into that fiery cloud that Max created. Couldn't Ike have at least waited for a couple of minutes? Now she was probably going to be the topic of conversation without having had a chance to at least enjoy some of the mind-spinning effects.

"That's standing next to a dead man," Ike informed her, correcting her correction, "if you don't hurry up and start serving those spareribs soon." He glanced over his shoulder to the door and the saloon that lay beyond. "I've never seen such a surly bunch out there."

"Sure you have," Max scoffed. "That bunch only comes in two grades. Surly and surlier."

"Then they've gone down to a new low. Surliest," Ike told him. He looked over Lily's shoulder and breathed the aroma in deeply. He could feel his own taste buds begin to stir. "Anything I can do to help?" he asked Lily as she looked up at him. "Other than taking your place with the sheriff here?"

She felt herself blushing and turned back toward the pot again. Hoping that the men would attribute the red color in her cheeks to the heat coming from the burner rather than the heat coming from within her.

"All right," she told him, giving the pot closest to her a last stir, "I need willing hands. The ribs are ready to go."

Ike went over to the cupboard and got down the first stack of dishes. "Great, because every mother's son of them has put in for double orders." He put the dishes down on the counter. "There's going to be enough money flowing out there to help feather the new restaurant fund."

This was the first she'd heard of that. "What new restaurant fund?" Lily wanted to know.

"Town's growing," was all Ike said as he returned to the cupboard for a second stack of dishes.

She looked to Max for an explanation. She was sure Alison would have mentioned something to her if they were thinking of building a restaurant. Both her sister and her brother were trying subtly and not so subtly to convince her to stay in Hades. As if.

"Ike and Luc have become Hades's resident entrepreneurs," Max told her when Ike said nothing. As Lily placed an order on a plate, he moved the plate to the rear, creating a manual assembly line for her. "They started out by buying the Salty, then the general store, then brought back the movie theater."

Ike set down a third stack of dishes beside the other two. He was going to have to get Isaac back in here to wash dishes, he calculated, if they were going to have enough clean plates to go around. He wondered if Luc would mind going to his house and rounding up some more flatware.

"Been thinking on this for a while now," Ike confessed. "I figure it's time to build someplace for the citizens to go and have a little atmosphere with their meals, other than staring at a moose head, of course," he laughed, referring to the one that had come with the place when he and Luc had purchased the Salty. He pinned her with a look. "Know where I can find myself a good chef, darlin'?"

With Ike, it was hard to tell when he was putting her on. But that didn't seem to be the case right now. "You're serious."

He winked at her in response, then confided,

"Don't let this smile fool you, darlin', I've got my serious moments. Just ask my wife."

Serious or not, it made no difference in her life, Lily thought, fishing more spareribs out of the pot and placing them on the nearest plate.

"No," she replied. "I don't know where you can find a good chef. But I'll ask around for you when I get back to Seattle."

She was leaving, Max thought.

Of course he'd known it all along, had never thought anything else, yet hearing Lily say it so casually made something inside his gut tighten. For the first time, he realized what his mother must have felt like, anticipating his father's imminent departure. Wayne Yearling talked about leaving Hades incessantly and there'd never been any reason for her to doubt that he would, even though they'd created together three children. No reason but hope.

He knew where things like that led. Nowhere.

His hands filled with plates, his back against the swinging door, Ike noticed the look on Max's face and wondered how long it would take two intelligent people to reach the conclusion that had occurred to him right from the start. With a shake of his head, he went out into the main room.

The moment Lily came through the swinging doors several minutes later, a cheer went up. It had less than a second to sink in before she was being hoisted onto the broad shoulders of two robust, heavy-set lumberjacks who towered over the crowd.

She squealed with surprise as she suddenly found

herself six feet off the ground. Twisting around, she looked down at Max with a touch of panic in her eyes.

"I think they want to show their appreciation," Max shouted over the din.

Lily grabbed a fistful of each man's shirt, sure that she would fall off if she didn't. "How, by getting me airsick?"

He heard a touch of nervousness in her laughter. He knew the men meant well, but he didn't want her spooked. Time to ride to the rescue. "Let the lady down, Ivan, Klaus," he told the two men.

Like oversize children whose fun had been curtailed, the two giants reluctantly complied. The next moment they turned their attention to acquiring second helpings.

Hands filled with bills began coming at him from all sides. Ike couldn't put the money into the register fast enough as the men chowed down. His eyes met Lily's across the counter. "Sure I can't make you an offer you can't refuse?"

A smile curved her mouth. She had to admit she'd never had such a rewarding hands-on experience, even counting the best night they'd had at *Lily's*. But her life, her career—not to mention the restaurant she'd worked so hard to make a go of—was back in Seattle, not here. She had to remember that.

Lily nodded and mouthed, "I'm sure," knowing that there was no way he could possibly hear her answer amid all the noise.

"Lily!"

Lily looked around. She'd heard her name shouted,

but hadn't a clue which direction the voice had come from. Standing beside her, Max placed his hand on top of her head and turned it to the left of the room. "That way," he told her.

She saw Jimmy coming toward her. April was nowhere to be seen, but there was a rather distraught-looking older woman plowing through the crowd with him. It looked to Lily as if he was coaxing her along.

Reaching her, he made the introductions. "Lil, this is Gracie Witherspoon. She has a problem I think you might be able to help her with."

Confused, Lily looked at the woman. Now what? "Hello."

The woman appeared to be torn between being embarrassed and distraught. The words fairly burst out of her mouth. "Bambi's wedding is the day after tomorrow."

"Bambi?" Lily looked from her brother to Max. Was the woman talking about a pet? Was she marrying off some prized dog or horse? At this point, Lily didn't think she'd put anything past the citizens of Hades. People did some pretty strange things when they were lonely or bored and generally isolated.

"Her daughter," Max whispered in Lily's ear.

Despite the warmth in the room and the press of bodies, the feel of his breath along her neck made Lily shiver. Made her remember.

"And Ilka's got the flu."

Lily raised her brow as she looked at Jimmy. "Another daughter?"

"The woman who was supposed to help with the

cooking," Jimmy supplied. He'd been the one who had sent Ilka to her bed after examining her. Gracie Witherspoon had descended upon him within the half hour with much gnashing of teeth and wringing of hands.

The light bulb in Lily's head went off. Cooking. Of course. That's all she seemed to be good for around here.

Well, why not? It was what she was good at, what she enjoyed doing, she reminded herself silently.

"And you need someone to prepare the food for the reception?"

Hope entered the sky-blue eyes as Gracie nodded vigorously, her gray hair becoming undone from its bun. "Yes. I can pay," she added quickly.

Probably not much and not anywhere near what she was accustomed to charging for catering weddings in Seattle, Lily thought. But then, she hadn't come here to make money, she'd come to try to revitalize something that felt as if it had died within her. Maybe this would help in the long run.

Just as making love with Max had in the short run.

"That's really not necessary," Lily told her. "Consider it my wedding present to your new son-in-law and your daughter." Try as she might, Lily couldn't get herself to wrap her tongue around the name Bambi and not laugh.

"I even got cayenne pepper," Gracie volunteered. "Ike said how you favor that."

Lily could only laugh as she looked over the woman's head at Ike.

"For spareribs, Ike, not unconditionally." She looked back at the hopeful, round face in front of her. Even if she'd been so inclined, it wasn't in her to say no. Not when she was faced with such unabashed hope. It wasn't every day a person got to play hero. "All right, Mrs. Witherspoon, tell your daughter she'll have her reception. I'll need to go over the list with you, find out how many people are coming—"

"The whole town," Gracie said quickly.

Great. I'll be cooking all day, Lily thought.

"All right, but I also need to know what you're planning on serving." Going full steam ahead, Lily suddenly stopped and looked at Ike. After all, he'd gotten her into this, it was up to him to help her. "I'm going to need someone to fly me to Anchorage and steer me to the grocery stores."

Though the request was directed at Ike, it was Max who answered. "I can probably get April to fill in for Sydney and have Sydney fly you to Anchorage. She does a lot of shopping for the people in the area, picking up things the general store doesn't carry, that kind of thing."

Lily nodded. "Sounds good."

She couldn't help noticing that Max hadn't volunteered to come along. Had her show of temper scared him off? Not that it mattered one way or another, she told herself. She'd be leaving soon and it looked as if she was going to be busy for the next couple of days. That left little time for them.

Or for her to make another mistake.

* * *

"Can't tell you how much I appreciate this."

Lily looked up from the plate she was preparing. Cooking was only half the battle with a catered affair. The rest of it was in making food look appealing. She placed a sprig of finely cut parsley on top of the scalloped potatoes. A carefully prepared pork chop shared the plate with the potatoes and glazed carrots.

It had taken her only one look at the previous menu to toss it out. Convincing Gracie to go along with the change had taken less time. The woman had given her carte blanche and stayed out of her way, other than to pay the tab for the food.

All of her catering jobs should go that smoothly, she thought.

"You don't have to," she told the woman. "I can see it in your face."

Impulsively, Gracie took Lily's hand and squeezed it. "You are a godsend."

No, Lily thought, an Allen-send. If she hadn't caught Allen in bed with that chicklet, she would have never come up here. At least, not any time soon. And Bambi Witherspoon's guests would have probably had burnt offerings to eat, if what she'd heard about Gracie Witherspoon's cooking was true.

"I'm only too happy to help," Lily assured the woman, taking back possession of her hand. "Dinner is almost ready," she promised.

Just as she said it, she heard someone come into the kitchen. Several someones. As she turned to look, she was surprised to see Max. In his wake were his sisters and sister-in-law, as well as their spouses, Luc, Ike and Jimmy.

The kitchen was already crowded with just Gracie and her standing in it. "Hey, there's not enough room in this kitchen," Lily protested.

"Don't worry, we're not staying," April promised. "We're here to help you bring all these plates out."

"Everyone's looking forward to this," Alison assured her.

"Jimmy told us how he got you into this," June, Max's younger sister, said. "The least we can do is help with the routine work—none of us can hold a candle to you when it comes to cooking."

"Especially June," Max quipped. "If it's not motor oil, she doesn't know what to do with it."

Lily looked at June. It seemed incongruous to her that someone who looked as pretty and delicate as June Yearling did could be the town's only mechanic, but Max had assured her that June would rather spend her day under the belly of a car, repairing it, than do almost anything else.

Kevin could use someone like that, she'd mused. His fleet of taxis were always in need of something.

"What do you want us to do?" Max was asking, presenting himself front and center.

Lily caught her breath, unaware that anyone else had heard her and missing the way Max's sisters exchanged looks. Lily knew exactly what she wanted him to do, but it didn't involve food, or an audience, both of which were here.

"Start taking them out." She pointed toward the

table. It was crowded with dishes that were covered with lids she'd purchased at a kitchen supply store Sydney had taken her to yesterday. With all this help, she wouldn't have to bother with the lids. Everyone was going to get a hot meal at the same time.

She smiled to herself as she watched the crew file by, each taking a dish. Less than modern conditions notwithstanding, it looked as if she was going to pull this off, after all. With a little help from the bride's mother's friends. And hers.

Like a prism that shone with captured sunlight, Lily's smile captivated Max, fascinated him. He didn't feel like filling his hands with plates of baby pork chops, julienned carrots and scalloped potatoes. He wanted to fill them with Lily. With the feel of her skin, the warmth of her body, the silkiness of her hair.

Coming close to her, he inclined his head and asked, "What?"

Blinking, she looked up at him, not realizing that she must have let her thoughts show.

"I feel a little like the sorcerer's apprentice." The scene with all the broomsticks carrying out buckets of water came to mind. Except instead of buckets of water, her broomsticks carried plates of food.

His eyes touched her. "Funny, I would have had you pegged for the sorcerer instead," Max said just as he filed by.

His comment lingering in his wake like a seductive melody; it took Lily a long moment to rouse herself and get back to work.

* * *

Rather than come out and mingle once dinner was served, Lily remained in the kitchen, putting the finishing touches on the wedding cake. She'd stayed up most of the night preparing it. She figured that if things went well, a woman only had one wedding cake in her life. It might as well be a work of art.

And Lily's was. But it had been touch-and-go for a while there.

Standing back, she allowed herself to drink in the sight and admire it before it was to be taken out to the garden to be claimed by the bridal couple.

"It's beautiful."

She smiled as she heard Max's voice behind her. The compliment pleased her. And she was quite in agreement with Max. Lily had never believed in false modesty.

"Thanks, I'm rather proud of it myself." Circling it slowly, she regarded the seven-tier cake critically and found nothing lacking. Thank God. "I haven't made a wedding cake since I can't remember when. I kept having this nightmare that it would turn out all lopsided and droopy."

He could see her concern, but it really wasn't warranted. Not with this crowd. "As long as it tastes good, I don't think anyone would notice if it was sinking in the middle."

The men might not, but she would have bet her restaurant that Gracie and her daughter would.

Lily turned to look at him, an amused smile playing on her lips. "Don't know very much about women, do you, Lawman?"

Max took that to be a challenge. One he meant to meet. "No, but I'm willing to learn."

Their eyes met for a long moment. She thought of the other night. He'd seemed to anticipate her every need before she was aware of it.

"Seems to me you're learning already and a damn fast study at that."

He took her into his arms. "Seems to me there's always room for improvement." His smile curled into her veins as he brought his mouth down to hers.

"Isn't this where I came in two days ago?" Ike asked, coming up behind them.

Max sighed mightily as he pulled his head back and looked at his friend.

"You do seem to have a problem with your timing, Ike." It was apparent that the man was not about to discreetly take his leave. Not that Max would have expected it. "What do you want?"

Ike was the soul of innocence as he approached the wedding cake. Admiration shone in his eyes as he looked at it and then its creator.

"Nice work," he told Lily in an aside, then turned to answer Max's question. "To help you roll in the cake—before it melts from the heat you two are generating."

Getting into the swing of the good-natured teasing, Lily waved the two men on their way. "Just take the cake out."

Bringing up the rear, Max paused to look at her. "Aren't you coming?"

Lily gestured around at the pots and pans that had

accumulated. She wasn't one of those people who cleaned as she went along. Hence it looked as if an aluminum war had been waged here.

"I have to clean up here—"

Nodding to Ike, Max figured the man could handle the cake on his own, at least as far as the edge of the house. He had something else to take care of.

"That is not part of the arrangement. You volunteered to cook, not to clean," he reminded her. "Seems to me you more than did your part."

Without waiting for an argument, Max threaded his fingers through hers and began to drag her out.

Lily caught her lip between her teeth, feeling guilty at the mess she left. "I like finishing what I start."

He looked at her significantly. "So do I."

Suddenly her heart had lodged itself in her throat. Lily half expected him to take her into his arms and kiss her again.

But instead, he pulled her out to the garden where the reception was being held. Stopping just short of the table where the cake now stood, Max moved behind her and tugged at her apron strings.

Her hands immediately went behind her to stop him. "What are you doing?"

She heard him chuckle behind her and felt a wave of heat wash over her. "Don't worry, the apron's the only thing coming off. For now," he added in a whisper against her ear.

The heat spread. "Oh?"

He turned her around to face him. "And only if you want it to." His hands on her hips, he stopped to cock his head, listening. "That's Jake Marley," he told her. "Lead guitar," he added when she looked at him quizzically. "The band's starting up again."

She was only vaguely aware of the outside music. There was a symphony playing in her head. It had started the moment he'd touched her.

"So?"

"So," he presented his hands to her, "I'd like this dance."

She realized that her mouth had dropped open and closed it again. "You dance?"

Dancing with her, he inclined his head. "On occasion. Don't look so surprised. I've been doing it ever since I learned how to walk upright and eat with a knife and fork instead of my hands."

She'd gone and done it again, stuck her foot in her mouth. Up to the thigh. "I didn't mean—"

"Yes, you did," he told her good-naturedly. "But that's okay, I'm getting used to it."

She sighed, knowing the fault lay with her, but she couldn't help it. "It's just that I don't have any expectations."

He supposed he could live with that. "That's what makes the surprises so nice," he told her, tugging her closer as the music played.

She resisted only for a moment, then let the music and the man take her away.

Stirred, Max found himself having to fight off the urge to press a kiss to her hair. "That was a very nice thing you did back there, helping out Gracie."

She shrugged. Cooking was as natural to her as

breathing. The feat hadn't been all that much, really. "I like coming to the rescue."

She felt the soft chuckle rumble in his chest before she heard it on his lips. "Looks like we have something in common."

Lily thought of the way he'd materialized out of nowhere, coming to her aid when the bear had chased her up the tree. "Maybe we do at that."

Leaning her face against his shoulder, she hid her smile.

And let it seep into her soul instead.

Chapter Fourteen

Until Lily had come into his life, Max wouldn't have believed that he could be moved by a woman to the point that he was contemplating forsaking everything just to be with her.

Since he was ten years old, he'd always tried his damnedest to avoid letting something like this overtake him. It was at ten that he'd seen firsthand what loving someone, *really* loving them, could do to a person. It could rob them of their reason, of their very will to live.

The way it had with his mother.

He couldn't allow that to happen.

Yet the thought of being without this woman who was sitting beside him in the Jeep as he drove through the darkness was like trying to close his hand over so many jagged shards of glass. The pain of it was beyond description.

It hurt too much to contemplate.

Max wasn't even sure just when or how this feeling had overtaken him, couldn't point to a single moment when his feelings had changed. He just knew they had.

But his will to survive was stronger, far stronger than his mother's had been and Max was determined not to become a shadow of the man he believed himself to be, the man he *had* to be, for his own sake as well as the sake of everyone who depended on him in this small town.

They were almost the last to leave the reception. Sydney had left to fly the happy couple to Anchorage for their honeymoon and the bride's mother had insisted on thanking Lily over and over again. Several people made it a point to tell her how they wished she would stay, how a restaurant was just the kind of thing that Hades needed.

She'd answered one and all with the same polite smile, saying that yes, it was, and saying nothing further.

She was going to leave.

In a week.

Seven days.

The thought lingered in his mind.

They were coming to a fork in the road. To get to his place, they needed to turn right. Left for hers.

Max turned toward her. She'd been unusually quiet this evening. "Want me to take you home?"

The question roused her. She'd been busy looking at the stars. And wrestling with her thoughts. "You mean Alison's house?"

Lily refused to refer to her sister's house as "home," even though she had actually begun to think of it that way. Had begun to think of Hades that way.

It was absurd, she chastised herself. Home was in Seattle. Home had always *been* Seattle. Just because two of her siblings lived here didn't suddenly make this place home.

She knew that wasn't the reason her heart was giving her trouble. Love made a place home. Contentment.

Damn, she was slipping again. Lily struggled to keep a tight rein on her thoughts, her feelings.

She realized Max was waiting for an answer. She turned her head toward him. "No."

Without a word, Max turned his vehicle to the right. Words didn't pass between them the rest of the way there. They didn't have to.

The moment the door to his cabin was closed behind him, Max took the woman he'd been aching for into his arms. His lips were quick to find hers.

The kiss, born of need, of desperation, exploded between them. It deepened instantly. Like two leaves cast adrift in a gale, they clung to one another, finding their worlds in each other.

It was easy to isolate herself, to not think beyond the moment. With only the moonlight pushing its way in through the uncovered windows, illuminating the dark, Lily felt herself safe from tomorrow, safe from yesterday.

The room tilted dangerously as she unleashed all the feelings that so dangerously threatened her own self-preservation. She didn't care about the heartache that waited for her, hiding behind the last day of the week, behind Saturday. Didn't care about the loneliness that would contrast so sharply with this feeling of joy that came from being here with him like this. She only wanted the feeling.

Her hands raced along his body, unbuttoning, tugging, tearing as he kissed her over and over again. Lily was desperate to absorb every nuance of the sensation until she felt drunk from it. Until she felt intoxicated with the power that coursed through her veins as the sounds of Max's sharp intake of breath wove its way into her consciousness.

She was stirring him.

Just as he was stirring her.

They barely made it three feet into the cabin, sinking onto the eight-by-ten rug that covered the scarred wooden floor, their bodies clinging to one another. Pledged to one another.

Max couldn't get enough of her.

Each kiss blossomed into the next one, increasing his hunger rather than appeasing it.

He kissed her everywhere, thrilling to the way she twisted and turned beneath his lips, the way she bucked when he found a particularly sensitive spot.

And all the while, his own excitement, his own

anticipation, continued to grow until it became a superhuman feat to hold it back.

He wasn't Superman, he'd never pretended to be. Just a man, a mortal man who wanted this woman more than he wanted anything else in his life.

Bracing himself above her, Max slid in, taking what he needed to survive, giving of himself to continue.

The sensations that had been teasing her, dancing to and fro at an ever-increasing tempo all rushed up at Lily as the final moment seized her.

Wrapping her legs around him, she cried out Max's name as she arched herself far off the floor.

And then she sank physically and emotionally back to the tiny space of earth she had occupied just a moment before eternity had ripped open its doors to her.

She doubted if she had ever been this content. This tired. This happy.

He wanted her this way forever. In his life. In his bed.

He knew it was impossible.

But still, he wanted her to know. Wanted to tell her what was in his heart here in this small cabin in the wilderness.

Rousing himself, Max raised up on his elbows. He framed Lily's face with his hands and looked down into her eyes. She had beautiful eyes, he thought. He could go on looking into them forever.

Could he see forever in them, *his* forever?

He didn't know.

"Lily—"

Her name lingered in the air as he searched for words that refused to present themselves. His mind refused to cooperate, going completely blank.

He felt like a tongue-tied idiot, not that he'd ever had a way with words. But he'd never been transformed into a mute before, either.

"What?" she coaxed, secretly wondering if she wanted to hear what he had to say.

No matter what it was.

Because whatever it was, whether to reinforce the thought that this was nothing more than a pleasant time for the two of them, or to state that it was *so* much more, carried consequences with it. Consequences she wasn't sure just how to face, or what to do with.

He began again, saying her name, getting no further. Afraid, she raised her head and just barely brushed her lips against his. It was all the encouragement he needed to abandon the statement that was forming so awkwardly on his lips.

And then, just as he took her into his arms again, he could hear banging just a few feet away. Someone was pounding on his door.

Vanessa? Damn, he hoped not.

"If it's Vanessa—" he warned angrily under his breath, reaching for his pants.

He'd done all he could to keep her away from him, to make her understand why there could never be anything between them beyond the friendship of a sheriff for one of the people of his town.

"Sheriff, you in there? I saw your Jeep parked out here. Open up, I gotta talk to you!" Each word was punctuated with more banging. It was getting louder, more insistent.

Recognizing the voice, Max sprang to his feet. Taking her hand in his, he helped her up, then gathered her clothes.

"Go into the other room," he ordered, pushing her things into her arms.

The last thing he wanted was for Lily to be the subject of cruel speculation. He quickly pulled on his pants, then looked over his shoulder to make sure that Lily was out of the room and safely hidden. Only when he saw the bedroom door close did he unlock the front door to admit Vanessa's father.

He saw instantly that the tall, rangy man was unsteady on his feet. It was a familiar condition.

"She's gone," Ulrich announced to the world at large. He waved a crumpled sheet of paper in front of Max. "She's run off. Here!" Vanessa's father thrust the paper into his hands.

The cloud of alcoholic vapor that accompanied the statement was pungent and overwhelming. Momentarily holding his breath, Max turned on the light. He quickly scanned the note. Written in pencil, the words were hardly visible. But he read enough.

"We had an argument," the man whimpered, collapsing onto the sofa, vacillating between despair and anger.

"Stay here, Mr. Ulrich." Turning from him, Max saw his shirt and picked it up. "I'll call someone to

come and take you home. I'll go look for her.'' Max
shrugged into his shirt, rebuttoning it. ''And when I
find her, we'll sort this all out.''

But when he turned around, Max saw that Vanessa's father had passed out on the sofa. The way
the man did most nights, he'd heard.

Max shook his head at the pathetic sight. ''Just as
well.'' He had a feeling that the man would only
hinder him.

Max heard the door to his bedroom. He turned to
see Lily coming out. She was dressed again.

Lily nodded toward the slumped figure on the sofa.
''I heard.''

Then there was no need to waste time explaining.
Sitting on the arm of the sofa, Max pulled on one
boot, then the other. ''Call your brother, have him
take you and Sleeping Beauty here home.''

''I'll call Jimmy,'' she agreed, ''but he'll only be
taking Vanessa's father home. I'm going with you.''

''Lily—''

She knew he was going to try to talk her out of it,
but she could help. She wouldn't have offered if she
couldn't.

''If she's run off, Vanessa's a distraught young
woman. I've been there,'' she confided. And maybe
someday she'd tell him the details, but not now.
''Maybe I can talk some sense into her.''

To argue would be to waste time and every moment was precious. It was too dark to follow a trail,
just a hunch.

Max relented. ''All right. Let's go.''

Taking out her cell phone, she hurried to keep up with Max as they went outside. Two minutes later, Jimmy had been called and dispatched to Max's cabin to transport Vanessa's father.

Lily buckled up in the passenger seat. "You have any idea where she could have gone?"

"Some."

Putting the key into the ignition, Max took Vanessa's note out of his breast pocket and passed it to Lily.

Lily angled for light from the overhead map light and scanned the note. It was short and painful. Vanessa had written that she knew no one loved her and that she was going to kill herself to put everyone out of her misery.

Max waited until Lily put the note down in her lap. She looked, he felt, as if the despair in the note had gotten to her.

"Before my father left, my family lived in a little cabin just north of here. Vanessa knew about it. She once said that she thought it would be a nice place for a couple to make a start."

There was no need to read between the lines. The message was ten feet tall. "She meant you and her."

He nodded grimly. "Yes."

Max fervently hoped he was right. Because if he wasn't, he hadn't a clue where to look for Vanessa before dawn lit the sky and he could try tracking her.

The old cabin, which had once been instrumental in saving April and Jimmy when they had gotten caught in a freak June snowstorm while returning from the Inuit village, was far from the town proper. It felt even farther to him in the dead of night.

But the trip had been worth it. His hunch had panned out.

They found Vanessa's second-hand Jeep lying on its side in front of the decaying cabin. By the looks of it, it had been deliberately flipped over by someone with a death wish. But there was no sign of blood, no sign of Vanessa.

"Looks like you're right," Lily said to him as Max brought his vehicle to a stop beside Vanessa's. He pulled up the hand brake and unbuckled.

"Hope I'm not right about the rest of it," he murmured, looking around as he got out.

What he was afraid of was that Vanessa had chosen this place to commit her final act of defiance. To teach him a lesson.

Suicide was an ugly word, an abomination against God and man and such a waste, he thought.

The door was locked when he tried it. Max frowned. It was never locked. His family hadn't even locked it when they lived here.

Something was wrong, he could feel it in his gut. Fisting his hand, he pounded on the door just as her father had on his door less than an hour ago.

"Vanessa, open up."

He listened against the door, but there was no sound of movement from within the cabin. Max tried the doorknob again, but the lock didn't give. Taking his service revolver out, he raised his free hand to push Lily away.

"Stay back," he ordered just before he shot at the lock. The wood all around it splintered. Satisfied, Max tried the doorknob again. This time, it gave.

Rushing inside, they found Vanessa lying on the floor in front of the fireplace. Blood was dripping from each wrist. She'd slashed them.

The moment Lily saw the girl lying so still, so pale, she began ripping off the edge of her blouse.

Max looked at her sharply as he checked Vanessa's neck for signs of a pulse. He found a very faint one. "What the hell are you doing?"

"We have to bandage her wrists, stop the bleeding." She was turning her designer silk blouse into tatters. Lily looked around the room. "Is there any running water in here?"

"In the kitchen." The pipes leading to the sink in the bathroom had burst a long time ago.

"Go run it," she told him. "Make the water as cold as you possibly can." If this was winter, she would have sent him out front to gather snow, but this was the best they could do. "I need to dunk her wrists into cold water first, to slow down the bleeding. Then I can bandage her wrists."

Bending over the unconscious girl, Lily eased first one eye open, then the other, using her thumb and forefinger against each lid.

"Vanessa, can you hear me? Vanessa, it's Max, Max is here." She saw no point in drawing attention to herself. After all, the girl saw her as unfair competition. "Open your eyes and look at him, honey," she coaxed.

"I don't—"

Max stopped midprotest. Looking down at Vanessa's eyelids, he detected the faintest of flutters.

"You're not going to be able to get her there yourself. I'll take her, you run the water."

Scooping the girl into his arms, Max carried Vanessa into the kitchen while Lily hurried after him. Reaching the kitchen, she darted in front of him and turned the water on full-blast to cold.

"Hold her up," she instructed.

Working as quickly as she could, Lily bathed the slash wound on each wrist. As the blood was washed away, Lily sighed. He heard relief in the sound and raised a brow in silent query.

"It's a pretty botched job, really," she told him, pleased that the girl hadn't been adept at this. If Vanessa had been, she probably would have been dead by now. "She's going to be all right." Lily leaned her head in closer to the girl. "Hear that, Juliet? You're not dead. You get to live and look for a Romeo of your own."

Max carried Vanessa back to the living room where he set her down on the sofa and watched as Lily bandaged both the girl's wrists. Her movements, he marveled, were swift, competent.

"Where did you—"

She laughed, finishing off her handiwork. Just in time, too, she thought. If she had to rip any more silk from her blouse, she would have had to return home wearing only her bra.

"You can't live with two people studying medicine without learning something. I used to quiz Jimmy, and Alison used to use me as her dummy whenever she needed to practice her bandaging techniques." There was pure satisfaction in her smile as she looked at Vanessa's pink-wrapped wrists. "Guess it paid off."

Taking out her cell phone, she glanced to see if the signal was registering. It wasn't. With a sigh, she flipped it closed again. "Looks like we can't call ahead from here and warn Jimmy that we'll be needing his services again."

He scooped the girl up into his arms. "Maybe we can pick it up on our way into town." Max nodded toward the door. "Let's go."

"You know, you're pretty remarkable," Max told her much later.

The sun was beginning to debate coming up. They had brought Vanessa to the clinic, finally managing to call Jimmy from the road. He met them there and had taken over, after telling Lily that she had probably saved Vanessa's life.

Max's praise warmed her the way no sun could have. "Nothing your average superwoman couldn't do." The smile on her lips grew tight as she thought of the unconscious girl they had left in Jimmy's care. She remembered what it had been like to be filled with despair. Her parents' deaths had left her that way. But she had had Kevin to help her over the rough patches. And even Jimmy and Alison had each tried their best to get her to come around.

What would it be like, without anyone? "That poor girl—"

He knew where she was going with this. "Vanessa needs to get out of Hades, make a fresh start."

An idea occurred to her. Lily looked at him. "If she wants to come to Seattle, I could help her find a place there. She could even work at the restaurant until she found something more to her liking." She was pretty sure the girl wouldn't want to remain in her debt for too long. She knew pride when she saw it.

Max looked at her in surprise. "You'd do that for her?"

Lily saw no reason for his surprise. "Sure. Why not?"

"Like I said," Max repeated as he brought Lily up to her sister's door, just before he kissed her goodnight, "remarkable." And what made it even more so was that she didn't realize it.

But he didn't say what was preying on his mind, what had been underscored by her cavalier mention of her restaurant in Seattle. She was willing to take the girl with her when she went back.

She was going back.

More than that, she was leaving him.

But what did he expect? For her to remain here? It would make more sense, the idea of the restaurant notwithstanding, if he tried to make a life for himself in Lily's world. After all, they had policemen in Seattle. He could always find a career in law enforcement.

But for that to happen, he would have to leave everyone and everything he knew, leave behind a hole until the town found someone to take his place. And he would be doing it all because of Lily.

Hell, Max thought, dragging his hand through his hair as he walked back to his Jeep. He was taking a hell of a lot for granted.

He hadn't even told her how he felt.

For that matter, she might not even feel the way he did. Might not think the earth moved every time they came together. He had been her first, what gave him the right to assume he would be her last?

He had a week left. A week in which not to think about it.

A week before he had to think about it.

With renewed determination, Max pushed the thought out of his mind and drove home.

Chapter Fifteen

He'd never known a week to fly by so fast.

Looking back, it all seemed like a blur now. Seven days and nights flowing up into one another, forming an endless stream. He'd spent most of his time away from work with Lily, telling himself that all this was fleeting, without strings. Just a very pleasant time with an exciting, stirring woman.

Telling himself lies.

He'd never been much good at lying, even to himself. Maybe especially to himself.

They faced life together in those seven days. Vanessa had been treated and released. He'd seen Lily talking to her, giving her a check to help pay the girl's flight to Seattle when she was ready, promising her a job when she was. Vanessa said she'd be ready in less than two weeks. Lily had said she'd be waiting.

Now that the day had arrived for Lily's departure, he was no closer to a solution than he had been seven days ago. No closer to knowing how she really felt about him.

Oh, he knew that they were good in bed together. Didn't take a brain surgeon to figure that part out. She was attracted to him and he to her. But magnets and metal attracted, they didn't necessary build a future together or have feelings for each other.

And he didn't know how she felt about him, not really. A man couldn't come out and ask those kinds of things and saying those kinds of things was completely beyond his scope. It was as if he came down with lockjaw every time he even thought about saying something to Lily that remotely had to do with his feelings for her, or asking her to think about staying.

He glanced at the clock on the back wall above the bulletin board with its handful of Wanted posters and public notices.

She was leaving in ten minutes.

Leaving Hades, leaving Alaska.

Leaving him.

He continued to sit where he was, wishing he could focus on something other than the dark loneliness that was beginning to take huge holes out of his gut.

His sister June walked in, cleaning her hands on a rag that had once been part of a bright red dress. She was wearing her usual navy-blue coveralls with the by-now off-white racing strip running boldly across it. Three years his junior, she ran Hades's most successful—and only—garage and repair shop.

She closed the door with her elbow and crossed to his desk.

"You're all set, Max. It was just a leaky valve. *This* time," she emphasized. Ordinarily detail-oriented, Max had almost run the vehicle into the ground. It wasn't like him and she wondered if something was going on that she should know about. "I want to see that car of yours for a regular checkup by the end of next week, so we can get a jump on anything else that might be going wrong." She studied his face covertly. "It's not a colt anymore, you know, Max. That stallion's been around the state a few times."

Pausing to stick the rag back into her rear pocket, June decided to take her chances and comment on his expression. There was nothing Max hated more than having her meddle in his life. Nevertheless, she did it whenever she thought it prudent.

"All right, what's on your mind, big brother?"

He waved her question away. "Just woolgathering," he muttered.

Yeah, right, and she had a hunch she knew just where this particular skein of wool had originated. "Tucking that wool around a certain lady who's leaving today?"

He looked at her sharply, then willed the tension he felt to leave his shoulders. Funny how he had to keep telling himself to do that. He wasn't ordinarily uptight at all. But things had changed these past two weeks. And none of it, he thought, for the better.

"No."

June perched on the edge of his desk, leaning over so that her face was level with his.

"Never lie to your priest, your doctor or your mechanic," she told him cheerfully. "There's nothing wrong with caring for somebody."

He began to shuffle papers on his desk, just to have something to do. He hadn't a clue what it was he was moving from one spot to the other.

"There is if there's part of a continent between you. And there will be by tonight."

But there was a way around this, she thought. Surely he had to see that. "So? Ask her to stay."

He pushed himself away from his desk with the tip of his boot. The chair rolled backward, stopping at the wall. "It's not that simple."

June scooted forward to get closer. "Why? Don't you have feelings for her?"

He frowned at the crease her movement had made on his blotter. "Don't you have a timing belt to replace or a battery to jump?"

She sighed, getting off the desk. The man could be so damn stubborn.

"Never was any telling you anything." Taking a few steps toward the door, June stopped and looked at him. "But if you ask me—"

Max was right behind her. Hands to her back, he pushed her out the door.

"I didn't." With that, he closed the door.

"My bill will be in the mail," he heard her call through the door.

He merely shook his head and went back to his

desk. Work was waiting for him, though it would certainly keep. There was nothing urgent to take him away, either physically or mentally.

That was just the trouble.

Part of him wanted to stop at Alison's to see Lily one last time. To say goodbye. To hold her again, the way he had last night. To remember last night and the time they had spent together, exploring their bodies while trying to leave their souls out of it.

But he knew if he did go to Alison's house to see Lily before she left, he would probably do something stupid. Such as ask her to stay.

And if she refused, he wasn't sure how he would handle that.

He wasn't his mother, but the pain, he knew, would be difficult to deal with. Better to leave the request unspoken.

He glanced at his watch. It was two minutes faster than the clock above the bulletin board. He felt his heart constrict. Sydney would probably be taking off with Lily in a few minutes. The flight from Anchorage wasn't for another two hours, but Sydney never liked to cut things close. There was no way he could make it to the house now, unless he called.

Looking at the telephone for a long moment, he left the receiver where it was. In its cradle. Instead, he got up out of his chair and walked out of the office, to the Jeep his sister had just been working on.

There was someplace he had to be.

Max drove into the woods. He was going to the lake, the lake where he had first admitted to himself that there were the greenest shoots of feelings within him.

Stopping the vehicle, he quickly got out and went to the clearing. There he stood and waited until he heard the roar of the single-engine Cessna.

When it passed overhead, he took off his hat, shaded his eyes and said his goodbyes.

It was safer that way.

He hadn't come.

Lily couldn't believe it, but Max hadn't come. Hadn't come to say goodbye. She'd strained her ears, listening for the sound of his car, hoping against hope.

Being stupid.

She'd had an uneasy feeling last night, when he'd brought her home after they'd made love in his cabin, that this was the last time she would ever see him. She'd spent the entire evening battling against the sinking feeling, telling herself it didn't matter.

Lying to herself.

Because throughout the evening, she'd kept waiting for Max to ask her to stay. Waiting for him to say something, anything, that could be construed as an effort to induce her to change her mind about leaving.

But he hadn't.

It was as if he'd wanted her to go. Actions spoke louder than words, didn't they? And he hadn't come.

They'd talked about nonsense, making small talk, suddenly behaving like two strangers stuck in an elevator together, waiting to be rescued. And all the while, all she'd wanted was for him to sweep her into his arms and make some kind of half statement that he cared about her, even a little, that he'd miss her, even the tiniest bit.

But he hadn't.

He'd said nothing except to agree that Arthur would be relieved to see her and that her cell phone bill was probably going to rival the national debt by the time she set foot in Seattle. When she'd pointed out that Arthur's phone calls had become less frequent, Max hadn't taken the hint, hadn't said that maybe she could extend her stay a little while now that Arthur was handling things.

Her blood began to boil just thinking about it. How thick could one man be?

Unless, of course, that man didn't care.

Sadness drenched her as the small plane climbed higher above the clouds. Any doubts she'd had that he didn't care were just erased when Max failed to come by to tell her goodbye.

Almost everyone else in the town had come. Men she hardly knew, except by sight, had stopped at Alison and Luc's house this morning, interrupting her packing and wanting to know when she would return.

Gracie Whitherspoon had even come by to give her a shawl she'd just finished making and once again to express her undying gratitude. The woman was almost a complete stranger, but she'd come.

And Max hadn't, damn him.

The hell with him, Lily thought fiercely, clamping her hands onto the armrests. The hell with all men.

She wasn't about to get caught up in her father's trap, wasn't going to care so much that she ceased to function properly. Wasn't going to care so much that her health suffered.

She was going to be just fine, damn Max Yearling's insufferable hide.

"You're going to rip out my armrests," Sydney commented gently. She glanced at her passenger's face. "Can't be my flying, you don't look petrified. You look angry."

Lily shrugged, turning her face toward the window. Looking at clouds. "Just thinking."

Sydney laughed softly to herself. *Been there, done that.* "Men can be pretty damn soul-wearying at times, can't they?"

"Yeah." She turned to look at the other woman, embarrassed. "I mean, I wouldn't know."

Sydney smiled to herself. Lily still seemed unwilling to be open about what the rest of the town knew was happening. That she and Max were in a relationship whether either of them admitted it or not.

"All right," she said gamely, "take it from me. They can be." And then she smiled, thinking about Shayne, about how much happier her life was now than it ever had been. She'd found her purpose out here. And her heart. "But they're the best game in town."

"I wouldn't know about that," Lily mumbled under her breath.

But she would, Sydney thought. Unless she missed

her guess, Lily would. "So," she began cheerfully, "when are you coming back?"

Lily set her mouth grimly. She wanted to say "never" but this was where Jimmy and Alison lived. The possibility existed that she would return someday. "Not for quite some time."

Sydney's smile deepened. She wasn't about to take any bets on that.

Annoyed, Lily let the phone receiver slip from her fingers and hit the cradle with a thud. She'd just gotten off the line with one of her suppliers over an inventory error. *Her* error.

That was the third order she'd messed up in two weeks. This morning, when the man at the docks told her that there was going to be an increase in the price this month, she'd almost cried.

Damn it, why couldn't she get herself back on the track? Why was she letting some Neanderthal lawman mess up her mind so that she couldn't function right?

Lord knew she certainly hadn't left any sort of an impression on him.

He hadn't called her, hadn't written, nothing. It was as if those two weeks they'd spent together hadn't happened, as if what they'd had hadn't even existed.

Well, what had they had? she demanded silently, flipping on the computer on her desk. Great sex, right?

No, it had been more than that. At least, for her. It had been something wonderful.

She waited for the monitor to brighten. It didn't.

Now what? Realizing that she'd failed to turn it on didn't improve her mood.

And just how did she know it was "something wonderful"? she challenged herself. It wasn't as if she'd been around the block a few times the way so many other women had. Hell, she hadn't even opened the damned door, except for this one time.

Still, a little voice whispered within her, *a woman just knew.*

Or was that a myth, too?

The whole internal debate was getting to be too much for her. Swallowing an oath, she reached for her steadily dwindling supply of aspirin. She needed something to do battle with the raging headache she was getting.

"You know, maybe I should buy stock in that company. The way you pop those aspirins, dry even—" Arthur shivered, standing in the doorway "—you'd think they were going out of style."

She looked up at him accusingly. Lately, Arthur seemed to be hovering over her like a mother hen rather than a frightened chick. He'd gained confidence. At least her two weeks away had done someone some good, she thought darkly.

It had helped Vanessa, too, she reminded herself. The girl had taken her at her word and shown up at the beginning of this week. She was now working at the restaurant as a waitress and seemed a great deal happier than she had been.

Too bad the same couldn't be said for her, Lily thought.

"The only things going out of style are manners." Her tone, like her gaze, left no room for doubt. "Such as invasion of privacy."

"I'm not invading," Arthur replied with a proprietary sniff. "I've got a beachhead all stacked out here, remember?"

She sat back in her chair, waiting for the aspirin to kick in and kick butt. The headache was a killer. "You've certainly gotten cocky since I went on vacation."

"And you've certainly gotten surly," he countered. As he spoke, he began straightening things on her desk. A poster boy for nervous energy, Arthur's long, aristocratic fingers were never still for more than a second at a time. "Remind me never to let you leave again."

He'd been making unwanted observations about her behavior ever since she'd gotten back. Her scowl darkened. "Did you come in here for a reason?"

"Yes, there's a man out front who says he wants to talk to you about a social event." He pointed behind him toward the doorway for emphasis.

Lily sighed. The little drummers in her head were starting on their second set and she just wasn't up to pretending she cared about anyone's centerpiece arrangements.

She waved him out the door. "You handle it."

To her surprise, Arthur remained where he was. "Sorry, no can do. I already offered. He says he'll only talk to you. Besides, he's kind of cute." Arthur winked at her slyly. "Might be just what you need."

She was tired of advice, tired of everything. "What I need is an assistant who doesn't tell me what I need." Lily sighed, dropping her head between her hands as she tried to pull herself together. "All right, you win. Send him in."

She turned her chair toward the wall, taking in a deep cleansing breath and then letting it go again slowly before turning back toward the door.

Consequently, there was no air in her lungs for her to call on.

Her mouth dropped open as the man in her doorway walked into her office.

Max.

"You're the man with the social function?"

He felt like a man crossing the Grand Canyon on a tightrope. Riding a unicycle. In a strong tail wind. Not at all certain if he was going to live to make it to the other side.

He nodded in response to her question. "That's me."

"What kind of a social function?" Lily heard herself asking. It was a stupid question, but she couldn't seem to find her mind at the moment. It was gone and presumed missing.

His eyes never left her as he searched for some hint that he hadn't just made the biggest mistake of his life, coming out here like this. For all he knew, she'd patched things up with that bastard she'd been engaged to.

"That depends entirely on you."

He came. No matter what else was said, what else

happened, he came. A sudden surge of joy over-whelmed her. Before she could stop herself, Lily had cleared her desk and was launching herself into his arms.

The kiss could have melted steel and very nearly melted her.

But there were questions to ask, things to be made clear.

Beginning with her brain.

Lily wedged her hands against his chest, creating a small space between them as she looked up at Max.

"What are you doing here? Really," she empha-sized before he said something about the social func-tion again. They both knew he wasn't here to book a banquet room at *Lily's* for an Alaskan party.

He wanted just to be able to look at her. To stand here without saying a word and just look at her. "You might say I've run away from home."

Her brows pulled together in confusion. "I don't understand."

He laughed shortly as he shook his head. "I'm not sure I understand, either." For both their sakes, he voiced his thoughts out loud, trying to sort them out. "I've spent all my adult life not looking for a woman. Not letting myself get tangled up in anything but keeping the town safe for everyone in it." He sighed. "You changed all that."

Did he think that was a good thing, or a bad one? She couldn't tell from his expression. "Oh?"

"I didn't want you to," he told her honestly. "But

you did. You made me want things I didn't think I wanted.''

Hope began to jump in her stomach like tiny popcorn kernels in a heated pan. ''Such as?''

''A home, family,'' he enumerated. ''Kids. You.''

So far, it all sounded wonderful. ''Where does the running away part come in?''

Hands clasped together at the small of her back, Max tightened his hold, pulling her closer.

''Well, I figured we had a location problem and your commuting here every morning might be a problem, so I thought maybe I'd just come and live in Seattle, see how things went after a while.''

He made it sound as if he'd just walked across the street, rather than flown to Seattle from Anchorage. '''Things'?''

He nodded. ''You and me.''

She pressed her lips together, her eyes never leaving his. Following his lead, she laced her hands behind his back, as well. ''How are they supposed to go?''

He didn't want to talk, he wanted to kiss her again. To make love with her here, in this pristine office of hers. To sweep the computer to the floor with a single swing of his arm and take her here on her desk.

Instead he said, ''You tell me.''

''Damn it.'' Arthur's voice came through the open door from the hallway. ''Will one of you say I love you to the other and move this along?''

Stunned, Lily looked at Max, then toward the door. ''Arthur, you're eavesdropping.''

The disembodied voice took form as the tall, thin man stepped into the doorway. His hands were on his hips. "And it's a good thing I am because the way you two are pussyfooting around the subject, they'll be releasing *Jaws 57* before you get around to telling each other how you feel."

"Arthur," she ordered, pointing to the doorway behind him, "get out."

With a huff, the man turned on his heel and left.

"And close the door," Lily added.

A hand reached out and wrapped itself around the doorknob, pulling it closed.

Max looked at her, secretly happy about Arthur's prompting. "How do you feel?"

She caught her lip between her teeth, then said, "You first."

"I think that's evident by the fact that I was the one who came to you."

She knew that. And it warmed her heart. But she craved words. Wonderful words to play and replay in her mind for the years to come. When she looked back at all of this and how it had begun. "Tell me anyway. Maybe I need to hear it."

"I love you," he said softly. "I don't want to, but I do."

She pretended to frown. "Not very romantic."

"I can do better," he promised. Mischief glinted in his eyes. "After you have your turn." When she said nothing, he got just the slightest bit uneasy. "I'm out on a limb here, with my feelings all hanging out."

She laughed. Funny how she had never noticed that

he was really adorable before. She wondered if the people of Hades knew their sheriff was adorable. "Yes, you are."

Max squeezed her a little, holding her against him. "So?"

"So, all right. Uncle," she cried the way little kids used to when they gave up. "I love you, too." They heard a dramatic sigh coming from behind the door. Lily grinned as she looked up at Max. "I think we're a major disappointment to him."

"Right now, I don't really care." Arthur was the last thing on his mind. "Do you really love me?"

This time, there was no holding back, no safety net. This time, she took the leap, knowing she would catch the trapeze bar with both her hands.

"With all my heart." She bit her lower lip, saying what had been lingering on her mind these past two weeks. "I love you enough to try to make a go of that restaurant Ike was talking about building."

He hadn't thought she could surprise him, but she just had. "You're serious."

She nodded in reply and he hugged her. Hard. "Hell, if it doesn't do well, I can always resort to selling snow cones for half the year."

Pulling back his head, Max looked at her, wondering if she'd forgotten to factor in a very important detail. Her place of business was here. "What about *Lily's*?"

"I can open up *Lily's 2* in Hades. Leave Arthur in charge here. Come by a few times a year to see how things are going. Besides—'' Lily grinned, patting her pocket ''—there's always the cell phone.''

Max searched her face and knew that she wasn't just talking. She meant this. "You'd do that for me?"

"No," she answered quietly, her eyes on his. "I'd do that for me."

They thought they heard another sigh, a softer, deeper one this time, but they weren't sure. Besides, they were becoming far too busy to investigate at the moment.

*   *   *   *   *

*Silhouette presents an exciting
new continuity series:*

**When a royal family rolls out the red carpet
for love, power and deception, will their
lives change forever?**

The saga begins in April 2002 with:

The Princess Is Pregnant!

by Laurie Paige (SE #1459)

**May: THE PRINCESS AND THE DUKE by Allison Leigh
(SE #1465)**

**June: ROYAL PROTOCOL by Christine Flynn
(SE #1471)**

Be sure to catch all nine Crown and Glory stories: the first three appear in
Silhouette Special Edition, the next three continue in Silhouette Romance
and the saga concludes with three books in Silhouette Desire.

And be sure not to miss more royal stories,
from Silhouette Intimate Moments'

Romancing
the Crown,

running January through December.

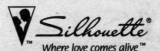